SPITFIRE!

With a deep coughing roar, the charge was detonated and the heavy ball of lead left the muzzle to plow into Auntie Mattie's torso.

Belle went in a rolling dive that took her to where Auntie Mattie had dropped her Colt. Closing her right hand around the ivory butt, she came to her knees. With her left hand joining her right, she faced the man and started to raise the short-barreled weapon. The move was as smoothly accomplished as if it had been practiced a great many times.

Trapped, the assassin let out a snarl of rage and raised his gun. . . .

OLE DEVIL'S HANDS AND FEET
WACO'S DEBT
THE HARD RIDERS
( )
THE FLOATING OUTFIT
APACHE RAMPAGE
THE RIO HONDO WAR
THE MAN FROM TEXAS
GUNSMOKE THUNDER
THE SMALL TEXAN
THE TOWN TAMERS
RETURN TO BACKSIGHT
WEDGE GOES TO ARIZONA
ARIZONA RANGE WAR
ARIZONA GUN LAW
( )

Waco series
WACO'S BADGE
SAGEBRUSH SLEUTH
ARIZONA RANGER
WACO RIDES IN
( )
THE DRIFTER
DOC LEROY, M.D.
HOUND DOG MAN

Calamity Jane series
TEXAS TRIO
COLD DECK, HOT LEAD
THE BULL WHIP BREED
TROUBLE TRAIL
THE COW THIEVES
THE HIDE AND HORN SALOON
CUT ONE, THEY ALL BLEED
CALAMITY SPELLS TROUBLE
WHITE STALLION, RED MARE
THE REMITTANCE KID
THE WHIP AND THE WAR
LANCE
THE BIG HUNT

Waxahachie Smith series
NO FINGER ON THE TRIGGER
SLIP GUN
( )
CURE THE TEXAS FEVER

Alvin Dustine "Cap" Fog series
ALVIN FOG, TEXAS RANGER
RAPIDO CLINT
THE JUSTICE OF COMPANY "Z"
( )
CAP FOG, TEXAS RANGER,
MEET MR. J.G. REEDER
THE RETURN OF RAPIDO CLINT
AND MR. J.G. REEDER
RAPIDO CLINT STRIKES BACK

The Rockabye County series
THE SIXTEEN DOLLAR
SHOOTER
THE LAWMEN OF
ROCKABYE COUNTY
THE SHERIFF OF
ROCKABYE COUNTY
THE PROFESSIONAL KILLERS
THE 1/4 SECOND DRAW
THE DEPUTIES
POINT OF CONTACT
THE OWLHOOT
RUN FOR THE BORDER
BAD HOMBRE
TEXAS TEAMWORK*

Bunduki series
BUNDUKI
BUNDUKI AND DAWN
SACRIFICE FOR THE
QUAGGA GOD
FEARLESS MASTER OF
THE JUNGLE

*   _Denotes title awaiting publication._
(   ) _Denotes position in which a proposed title will be placed._

MISSISSIPPI RAIDER

J. T. EDSON

A Dell Book

Published by
Dell Publishing
a division of
Bantam Doubleday Dell Publishing Group, Inc.
1540 Broadway
New York, New York 10036

ISBN: 0-440-22214-1

Printed in the United States of America

Published simultaneously in Canada

May 1996

10 9 8 7 6 5 4 3 2

OPM

For Joy, Marlene and Celia, the "Three Wise Monkeys" of my "spiritual" home, the Half Moon In Melton Mowbray, even though they don't care for Matilda the Hun

THE START OF THE LEGEND
How Belle Boyd Became the Rebel Spy
Author's Note

For the benefit of new readers, but to save our "old hands" from repetition, we have given a "potted biography" of Belle "the Rebel Spy" Boyd in the form of an Appendix.

When supplying us with the information from which we produce our books, one of the strictest rules imposed upon us by the present-day members of what we call the "Hardin, Fog and Blaze" clan and the "Counter" family is that we never under any circumstances disclose their true identities or their current whereabouts. Furthermore, we are instructed to *always* include sufficient inconsistencies to ensure neither can happen, even inadvertently.

We would like to emphasize that the names of people who appear in this volume are those supplied to us by our informants in Texas and any resemblance to those of other people, living or dead, is purely coincidental.

We realize that, in our present permissive society, we could use the actual profanities employed by various people in the narrative. However, unlike various other authors, we do not concede that a spurious desire to create "realism" is any excuse for doing so.

As we refuse to pander to the current trendy usage of the metric system, except when referring to the caliber of various firearms that had always been measured in millimeters—i.e., Walther P-38, 9mm—we will continue to employ miles, yards, feet, inches, pounds, and ounces when quoting distances and weights.

Lastly, and of the greatest importance, we must stress that the attitudes and speech of the characters is put down as would have been the case at the period of the narrative.

J.T. EDSON,
MELTON MOWBRAY,
Leics.,
England

CONTENTS

PART ONE

THE NEED TO KNOW

CHAPTER ONE

You're a *Woman*!

Rising slowly from behind a grove of royal and cabbage palms that grew on all sides of the fair-size clearing, the full moon caused their trunks to shine dim and ghostlike in its early rays. Overhead, almost at meridian, strange patterns of fluffy clouds billowed and the Seven Sisters (Pleiades) played hide-and-seek among swiftly moving, ever-changing thunderheads. From deep within the swampland to the right, the resounding voice of a great horned owl could be heard above the multitudinous croaking of bullfrogs. Every now and again, the deep belly grunt of a bull alligator echoed from the edge of a marshy watercourse nearby. Perhaps disturbed by the predator, a night heron glided above the treetops and its golden eyes flashed briefly in the glow of the small campfire in the center of the open ground before it vanished into the surrounding blackness. Insect noises in uncountable variety and locations floated on the gentle breeze. In the course of their nocturnal hunting, nighthawks banked and zoomed on silent wings. Also questing for food, an occasional leather-winged bat darted through a crazy pattern of flight in its efforts to catch black gnats or other of the tiny flying creatures drifting in swarms.

However, while conscious of the sounds, the half a dozen human beings gathered around the fire in the center of the open ground appeared to be paying little or no attention to them. Of different heights, builds, and ages, with one exception—whose headgear was black, broader-brimmed, and had a higher crown—the group wore white straw "planter's" hats, loose-fitting jackets over white shirts and silk cravats of various colors, and riding breeches tucked into the calf-high legs of their boots. Their attire and voices indicated they were well educated and wealthy Southrons, which was not surprising since they were in the woodland fringing the Mississippi River at Baton Bayou Parish, Louisiana.

Despite the situation between politicians from both sides of the Mason-Dixon line being grave, with much talk of the Southern states seceding from the Union because of what were clearly irreconcilable differences upon many issues—as was allowed in the Constitution—their main subject of discussion was the possibility of a good night's sport. In fact, the only reference to Yankees was when one of the group commented how little common sense or decent behavior could be expected from men who—instead of running their quarry for sport by night and allowing it to escape when cornered more times than otherwise, as was done in the South—set the hounds on its trail and selected places to lie in wait for it to pass, then, as so often happened due to the habit of both the red and gray species of fox when pursued to move in a circle around its normal domain, shot it.

Regardless of the comments upon the time of day selected by Yankees for hunting, because sport rather than acquiring a trophy and making an easy kill were the main incentives, throughout much of the South—especially from the late spring and summer months through to early fall—even early-morning hunting for a fox was rarely successful. This was because, as soon as the sun came up and caused the temperature to rise, conditions became too hot for the quarry, hounds, and horses to last long enough to make for a worthwhile chase.

At night, however, it was not unusual for a mature dog fox to run for three and a half to four hours before being caught and "treed." The term was particularly apt where the Southern gray fox was concerned. When hard-pressed and finding it was about to be caught, it would either climb into a leaning tree or go down a gopher hole. Although one was only rarely caught on the ground, unless it had developed the habit of feeding upon chickens and other small domesticated creatures, once treed the majority of them were left unharmed.

Suddenly, disturbing the man sprawled on the ground by its head, an unprepossessing-looking bay stallion "muck pony" tethered a short distance from the other mounts of the same strain gave a snort and gazed southward into the night.[1] At the same instant, the big bluetick coonhound acknowledged

[1] *Some of the events that occurred as a result of a proposal by the United States Cavalry to employ muck ponies in snow during winter campaigns*

as "strike dog" and leader of the pack by the other eight members of various breeds uncoiled from his sleeping position on the short grass. Rising swiftly to his feet, with his sensitive nose sniffing the night breeze, he stood tense and alert. Soundless though they were except for the inhaling of breath, his movements had the effect of bringing the rest of the hounds from their somnolent postures.[2]

"My ole Quincy hoss smells him a fox, or maybe a bobcat," commented the only member of the party not gathered around the fire, coming to his feet from where he had been sitting near the now-alert muck pony stallion and motioning with his head in its direction. Though tall, lean, and leathery faced, the way he was dressed and his voice suggested he came from a lower class of society than the others. His name was Joe Lassiter and he was the owner of the pack of hounds. Therefore, his words and actions brought silence, and turning his gaze to the bluetick, he continued just as quietly, "That ole Speed dog's got him the scent!"

Even as the words were being spoken, the sharp bark of a fox rang out from downwind. Instantly, Speed bounded forward with a bugle-voiced bawl that set the rest of the pack to duplicating his actions. Such was the speed of his actions, he hit the end of the leash that secured him to a bush and turned a complete flip. However, he came up immediately, baying furiously and trying to get free. Hurrying over while the hunters at the fire were rising, Lassiter started to liberate the hounds, commencing with Speed. The moment each was freed, it tore away with the speed of a frightened pronghorn antelope. By the time the last of the human beings was by his mount, which—like all the rest—had often been used for such hunting and showed agitation over the prospects suggested by the commotion, the wild and excited baying of the hounds was already a good half-mile away.

---

against the Indians on the Western frontier, but not the experiments themselves, are recorded in THE BULL WHIP BREED.

[2] *Descriptions of some of the breeds of dogs used for hunting raccoon and various animals, including some qualifying as big game, are given in* HOUND DOG MAN.

Having liberated the last of the pack, Lassiter strode swiftly to where his stallion was behaving in just as restive a fashion as the other horses. Bounding astride the blanket that served him as all the saddle he needed, he scooped up the reins of his Indian-style hackamore and, apparently all in one motion, set off. While far from a graceful-looking animal, the muck pony showed a surprising turn of speed. However, swiftly as it and its rider moved, the exception in the matter of attire was almost as rapid. Showing a deft ease that bespoke considerable experience in matters equestrian, the hunter in the black hat swung astride a dun gelding with lines indicative of a preponderance of American Five-Gaited Saddle-Horse blood and was away across the switch grass while the rest were still mounting. However, once they were on their horses, the others followed with alacrity and also displayed the skill at riding that almost every Southron of their class acquired.

Past the woodland fringing the river, much of the terrain over which the hunt showed signs of taking place was over hard-sand prairie covered with short switch grass, which would have offered a close-to-ideal footing for any type of riding horse. However, interspersed in various sizes and patterns across fair amounts of it were clumps of scrub palmetto, shallow lakes and ponds, hammocks—as the local population called hammocks of trees—sloughs and muck pockets making the surface quite treacherous to ride over at even a canter, although the muck ponies could handle it better than the other purebred breeds most wealthy Southrons rode at other times.

Guided by experience handed down from their predecessors in the sport of hunting at night as practiced in the Southern states, while following Lassiter at a fast trot, wherever possible the rest of the party rode more or less abreast instead of keeping to a single file. It had been found that doing so presented less chance of injury being sustained should there be a mishap. In case somebody's horse lost its footing and went down, there would not be an animal following that might step upon the rider or become entangled with the one lying on the ground. Therefore, at least in the early stages of the hunt before the quarry was set moving, the members of the party would try to allow each horse plenty of running room.

At a signal from their host, Vincent Charles Boyd—owner of the Baton Royale Manor plantation, within the bounds of which he maintained the less productive area as a place offering sport for his friends and neighbors—the party drew rein about two hundred yards from where the pack was busy attempting to get the track of their quarry lined out. Seeing where they were, the more knowledgeable followers informed the others that they would be in contention against Ole Silver Lightning, a dog-gray fox with a reputation for giving a good chase before contriving by some means to escape.

Showing their inherited great keenness and dedication to the task, every member of the pack was assiduously working a hammock offering thick cover. Cabbage palms, water oaks, a mixture of several scrub hardwoods, and a variety of vines made it hard for the pack to get the wily creature moving in a straight line. The scent was fresh and the anxious hounds, especially those younger and less experienced, tore through the heavy cover like mad things. For almost two minutes there was considerable confusion as members of the pack dashed here and there without achieving anything except raising a clamor with their eager voices.

Then, just as Lassiter was about to try to enforce some kind of order, the unmistakable bugle bawl of Speed sounded like a clarion to the north of the hammock. Instantly, recognizing the baying of their acknowledged leader, and being all too aware of what was portended by it, the rest of the pack almost literally tore holes through the vines inside the mound as they went rushing to join Speed. In a few seconds, more and more of them began to add to the clamor as they set off along the line the bluetick had discovered.

Having started to move as soon as they heard Speed's voice, the hunters cut around the side of the hammock.

No sooner had they arrived at the north side than the pack led by Speed jumped the fox as it was trying to sneak away undetected, and the chase was on in deadly earnest.

Judging by the response that came, the muck ponies, frequently used for such a purpose, seemed to enjoy the prospect of the chase and the wild music of the pack as much as did their riders.

Serving respectively as the master of hounds and chief whipper-in, Boyd and Lassiter were politely accorded the privilege of being the first off the mark. However, as at the camp, the slender figure with the black hat was next into motion by a slight amount. The speed with which the dun gelding took off, on receiving the signal to do so from the heels of boots that had no spurs as an added inducement, would have stood a good chance of dislodging a less competent rider. This did not occur, and, also contriving to remain mounted despite the display of energy with which the other close-to-frantically-eager muck ponies also responded to the sounds they knew so well, the rest of the party instinctively scattered to the right and left out in the wake of their three leaders and not one of them was more than a few yards to the rear.

"View halloo!" a young man making his first appearance at Boyd's plantation yelled incorrectly, as the fox was nowhere to be seen. The man was evidently seeking to prove he had ridden with more formally carried-out hunts that followed the lead of their English counterparts. "Tally ho! Yoicks!"

None of the other followers offered to raise any outcry or correct their companion. Instead, they—and he, to give him credit—concentrated upon what they were doing. There was plenty of open space in the terrain now being traversed, so the riders all allowed the enthusiastic animals to have their head. The ride to the hammock had been sufficient to warm up the horses, and they could run without the danger of pulling a tendon. However, swiftly as they were moving, there was no danger of their running in too close to the pack, which had been close to a quarter of a mile away when the chase commenced. A horse such as the muck pony could travel at a faster clip than any hound for a mile or so, but after that the positions were reversed and the pack slowly began to draw ahead.

For about an hour, although the real reason was that keeping to the fairly open switch-grass terrain was a benefit to its own running, Ole Silver Lightning seemed almost as if wanting to give its pursuers a chase to remember. However, with the hounds pressing, once again giving the impression of possessing tactical skill rather than merely acting upon instinct, it began to seek out much less easy ground through which to travel.

Because of the changed tactics, the dog-gray fox had succeeded in increasing the distance between itself and its human
pursuers—although the hounds were less affected—when the
hunt was approaching a narrow strip of scrub palmetto. Being
aware of the danger, Boyd, Lassiter, and the rider in the black
hat caused their mounts to slow to half speed before reaching
the treacherous footing and so were able to cross it without
mishap. Not so the rider to the left of the rough arrowhead
formation they had adopted. He had either failed to see or
underestimated the danger posed by the palmettos, so his horse
hit it at top speed.

Down went the animal as its feet slid from under it, its tail
pointed skyward. Showing great skill and presence of mind,
the young rider quit the saddle and sailed spread-eagled
through the air for about fifteen feet to land facedown and skid
onward a short distance in front of the upturned horse. Expecting him and his mount to be seriously injured, the latter
having turned a forward somersault and descended with its
head bent back beneath it, the rest of the party began to halt
their horses. Much to the relief of the other followers, both
made their feet after a few seconds. Except that they had col-
lected plenty of mud and, knuckling the sticky black goo and
water from his eyes, the man looked as if he had lain belly
first in a hog wallow, neither gave any indication of having
been hurt.

"Are you all right, Jubal?" Boyd inquired solicitously.

"I've felt better, Uncle Vincent," the young man replied
with a wry grin as he worked his limbs tentatively, then looked
to where Lassiter was restraining his mount's eagerness to resume the chase. "But nothing's broken. I'd better take my
horse back to the house, even though he won't be pleased
about that."

"Better luck next time," the tall, gray-haired, and distin-
guished-looking plantation owner commiserated. Cocking his
head, he listened to the fading sound of the hounds' trail music
for a moment and estimated they were at least a mile ahead
by now. "Let's go, the rest of you."

Watching his companions set off again, the young man who
might have counted himself fortunate to have escaped without
serious injury or even being killed gave a sign of disappoint-

ment. Then, adhering to the training in such matters he had
received from boyhood, he started on foot and, leading the
horse by the reins—which had been passed to him by Lassiter
prior to departure—proceeded in the direction of his uncle's
home.

On resuming the chase, the remaining members of the hunt
restrained their mounts and held the pace down to a medium
canter for around two miles. Then, at Boyd's signal, they
reined to a stop. Dropping from his saddle and allowing the
reins to dangle, knowing his unprepossessing bay stallion was
trained to stand still when this was done, Lassiter walked sufficiently far to prevent the breathing of the other horses from
interfering with his listening. At first he could hear nothing of
the hounds, but after about a minute he could make out the
deep resonant voice of Speed. With each passing second it
grew louder, and before long he could hear the rest of the
pack.

"Like I figured," the leathery-faced man declared, returning to the rest of the party and swinging into his saddle. "Ole
Silver Lightning's done got tired of being pushed that ways
and's coming back."

"Not straight back, though," replied the young follower
who had misused the hunting terms earlier. "I'd say he's
headed a considerable way to our right."

Grunting noncommittally, although willing to concede the
point—if only to himself—Lassiter started leading the way to
the east. While waiting until the condition of the rider and
mount that had taken the fall was known, the horses had had
time to catch their breath and were now anxious to go.
Therefore, they needed no encouragement to run swiftly in the
direction they were being guided. Then the route took them
into a wide and open grass-covered meadow partly surrounded
by scrub palmetto. Having advanced across it, they stopped
just short of the dense cover at the opposite side. From what
they heard, they could tell that the hounds were no more than
a couple of hundred yards to the north and coming directly
their way. Knowing his pack, Lassiter was aware that Speed
was still in the lead and closely followed by a redbone he
called Witch. That figured to him. The bluetick was a born
front-runner, but the bitch always liked to be up there too.

Suddenly there was a silver flash as the dog fox came out of the palmettos right among the hunters. Passing under the belly of Boyd's roan gelding, it continued across the clearing without breaking stride. Instantly, there was a jumble of horses as everyone tried to be the first to take up the pursuit. Having stopped a few yards behind the rest, the young man and the rider with the black hat were able to get clear before any of the others could extricate themselves for the chase, so the rest were left at the post. Being lighter and marginally the better in the saddle, the latter was slightly in the lead. In spite of that, such was the quality of Lassiter's stallion that it overtook them before they had passed the halfway mark on the open land.

Just what happened next was impossible to say. For some reason the stallion tried to shy away, and in doing so it went down. Unable to halt their rapid progress in time, the two closely following horses also were brought to the ground. However, the young man and the rider with the black hat could not duplicate the way in which Lassiter contrived to alight on his feet and run until gaining sufficient control to stop. Both of them went sprawling to the ground, with the latter twisting over and losing the headgear.

Alighting upon the other dismounted rider, despite the urgency of the situation, the young man began to get the impression that something was wrong. Much longer hair than he would have expected was brought into view by the loss of the hat, and there was something distinctly unusual about the face he saw being brought toward his. Of even greater importance, trying to break his fall and not descend heavily upon the other, his right hand came down upon the chest and felt something beneath the silk material of the shirt that most certainly could not have been present on a man.

"Well, I'll be eternally damned!" the young man croaked as he successfully prevented himself from completing the descent and rolled aside without making further contact. He noticed that all the horses, showing the resilience for which they were famed, were regaining their feet without showing signs of having sustained any serious injury. "You're a *woman*!"

"I never for a single minute doubted *that*!" replied the figure upon which the hunter had almost descended, speaking in a feminine Southern drawl that had the suggestion of her having had a good upbringing.

By the time the confusion caused by the accident was over, Ole Silver Lightning had found and ascended the leaning trunk of a scrub oak, which had too steep an incline for any of the hounds to follow. On finding their quarry had treed, the hunters gave him best and made no attempt to dislodge him.

"I'll shoot you, you wily ole son of a bitch, happen we lock horns again," Joe Lassiter threatened, but far from seriously, as was proved by his tossing down the carcass of a hen he had brought for the purpose. With the ritual over, he set off after the rest of the party.

CHAPTER TWO

Your Poppa Allus Wanted a *Son*

"**L**and's sakes a-mercy, Belle Boyd!" Martha Jonias groaned, rolling her eyes and gazing toward the ceiling as if in search of guidance and strength from the heavens. Framed by tightly curled hair that had become grizzled by the passing of many years, her normally pleasant and intelligent-looking black face showed a mixture of annoyance and resignation. Just under six feet in height, she looked almost as broad and round as she was long, yet the bulk was not formed by flabby fat. In addition to being firmly filled, the spotless white frock she was wearing had its sleeves rolled up to show well-muscled arms. "I surely don't know what I'm going to do with you. Almost your eighteenth birthday and still playing fool games like going a-hunting riding *astride* 'n' dressed as a *man*, for shame. Then coming home looking like you'd been rolled on by a hoss, which you nearly was."

"I've a full week to go before my birthday gets here, Auntie Mattie," replied the girl who had caused so much surprise for the first-time visitor to her father's Baton Royale Manor plantation a short while earlier. As the result of long experience, she showed no surprise over the extent of the woman's knowledge of what had taken place during the hunt. "Anyway, it will probably be the last time I get a chance to ride to hounds at night. From now on it will be by *daylight*—" The strongly emphasized word was accompanied by a shudder redolent of distaste. "Sidesaddle, all dainty and proper at that, but nowhere nearly so much *fun*."

Because of Ole Silver Lightning having treed and the three horses being shaken up by the fall, Vincent Boyd had decided there would not be any more hunting and the guests had gone with Joe Lassiter to return and attend to the needs of the muck ponies they had borrowed. She and her father had brought theirs to the mansion, but the head groom—who did not trust the task to anybody else, including his well-liked master and the daughter of the house, despite having taught her to be competent in that important part of the equestrian arts, even when they were only muck ponies and not what he regarded as being real bloodstock—had taken charge of them.

Knowing that the horse she had ridden for the hunt was in the best possible hands and would receive every care—or she would have insisted upon attending to its needs personally—the girl had sneaked into rather than just entered the house to which she would one day become the owner, according to her parents, without being asked by anyone what had taken place during the hunt. Given the connivance of her little colored maid, always a willing supporter in anything she did, she took a hot bath. Feeling sure her behavior would not be regarded with approval, she hoped to complete and change into more conventional attire before the woman who had been her nurse from the day she was born discovered she was on the premises. As had been the case so many times in the past when she had sought to conceal misbehavior from "Auntie Mattie," the attempt was not entirely successful. She had finished her ablutions uninterrupted, but found the old Negro woman waiting with obvious disapproval when she emerged from the bathroom.

If the young man who had come down from the horse and almost descended upon her had been able to see Belle Boyd at that moment, he would have been left with no doubts whatsoever with regard to her sex. She had just returned from the bathroom next door to the sitting room of her living quarters on the first floor of the mansion, her coal-black hair drawn tightly and bunched into a bun at the back of her head. In addition to her face being radiantly beautiful, albeit with more of a tan than was considered socially acceptable for one of her class and age, it had a suggestion of strength of will and intelligence beyond average. What was more, displayed because all she had on were white cotton pantalets—the ankle-long legs trimmed by blue lace—and heelless white slippers, the rest of her bodily contours ideally supplemented her features.

Five feet seven in height, the girl was far from flat-chested or skinny despite being slender. In fact, being so firm that the dark brown nipples were slightly uptilted, her breasts were

well developed for her age. Although not sufficiently to qualify
as being "hourglass" in lines, her torso slimmed at the waist
and opened out to curvaceous buttocks. Well-defined muscles
showed in her arms, and the graceful ease with which she
moved suggested that the same applied to her lower limbs. All
in all, she exuded a sense of controlled power and of being in
an excellent physical condition that was not a common trait—
or even considered necessary by the more conventional of their
peers—for members of her sex and age in the Southern states.

Some aspects of the room in which the conversation was
taking place gave indications of how unconventional was
Belle's upbringing and outlook. Its four-poster bed, the dressing table, wardrobe, and most of the other furniture and fittings
were such as might have been expected in any wealthy Southern household. However, there were intimations that its occupant did not conform strictly to the conventional dictates
Southron society expected of a well-bred and correctly raised
young woman.

One wall was lined with full-length mirrors, to which was
fitted the kind of horizontal wooden rail used in ballet schools
to not only allow limbering up and other exercises to be performed, but to let the one doing so see what was taking place.
As it had never been intended to help her attain a professional
career in even that highly regarded and generally considered
respectable section of the theater, such a fitment just qualified
as being socially acceptable. Less so was the well-polished
walnut box on the mantelpiece; it held a magnificent matched
brace of dueling pistols bearing the name of the renowned
master gunmaker Elijah Manton & Son of London, England,
along with a powder flask, bullet mold, and other items necessary for their loading and maintenance. Nor were the pair of
equally well-made *épée de combat* from the same illustrious
source, surmounted by a fencing mask, which formed a gleam-
ing cross on the wall above the fireplace, any more in keeping
with convention. At the other side of the room stood a dressmaker's dummy in the shape of a full-size female head and
torso, which was balanced upon a rounded base instead of the
more usual flat stand. However, as it was not intended to be
used for any kind of commercial purpose, it would just pass
muster as being permissible.

"*Fun!*" sniffed Auntie Mattie, knowing the reason for—if never having approved of—her unconventional upbringing.[1] "Your poppa allus wanted a *son*, and you've done everything you can to give him one, what with riding astride, shooting, fencing,'n' all the rest."

"Oh, come on, now," the girl requested with a smile. "I've *never* shirked my dancing lessons."

"You for surely never did, at that," Aunty Mattie admitted, but clearly with more reservation than approbation. "Only, it wasn't for *dancing* you took to 'em so good 'n' regular."

While the elderly Negress was speaking, Belle commenced a series of swiftly executed pirouettes that would not have disgraced many a professional ballet dancer. However, as she had deliberately elected to go in that direction, they were culminated by the delivery of a high kick that sent the sole of her left foot against the chin of the dressmaker's dummy and caused it to be rocked over. What was more, as it was pivoted erect again by its counterweighted base, she twirled gracefully and sent her other heel into the stomach area with equal rapidity, power, and precision.

"I've always believed a lady should know how to take care of herself in certain conditions," the girl remarked as she strolled with carefully assumed nonchalance toward the dressing table after having displayed an ability that any connoisseur of the art of French foot and fist boxing known as savate would have considered to be faultless in its execution.

"That's what the menfolks are for," Auntie Mattie declared. "They just natural' has to be good for *something*."

"I certainly hope it's for something a lot more than just *that*," Belle remarked as she sat down.

"What you *say*, gal!" Auntie Mattie protested, her always expressive face registering even greater disapproval than previously, although there was a faint twinkle suggestive of amusement in her eyes. "Was you younger, I'd have to wash your mouth out with soap and water for coming out with such talk. It all comes of you sitting 'round a fire out in the piney woods listening to them gentlemen you're with a-talking things

---

[1] *The reason for the unconventional education received by Belle Boyd is explained in the Appendix.*

a proper-raised young lady shouldn't understand, much less hear, while they's waiting for them fool hound dogs to find something to go chasing after.''

"I always cover my ears when they start," Belle asserted. "Like I've been taught is the *proper* thing for a young lady to do.''

"A proper-raised young lady wouldn't be out there anyways," Auntie Mattie countered. "Now get to putting on something more covering than you've got on now. Unless your daddy 'n' them's changed for the better right recent, which I don't reckon's likely to have happened, those gentlemen you've been out lallygagging in the piney woods with'll be coming 'round to have some food and do some bragging about their doings tonight's soon's they've finished tending to those fool muck ponies of Joe Lassiter's they've been using. Which, right now, you're not dressed fitten for mixed company, much's I conclude those young gentlemen's you've been out with'd like to see you this way.''

"Yes'm," the girl responded immediately, for while she might tease the elderly Negress—whom she gave an affection bettered only by that accorded to her parents—she would never have thought of disobeying.

"And there's something else for you to keep in mind, young lady,'' Auntie Mattie announced as Belle took the sleeveless white cotton chemise her maid had left on the dressing table and started to don it. Although it would not have been discernible to anybody who did not know her so well as did her ward, her voice had taken on a note of deadly serious warning as she watched what was being done. "Don't you go off running those two fool hound dogs of your'n on your lonesome in the piney woods at night for a spell.''

"Am I getting too old for *that* too?" the girl could not resist inquiring, despite having noticed the change of timbre in the elderly woman's voice.

"There's more to it than just that, although it'd be more'n enough most times," Auntie Mattie answered in the same soberly cautionary fashion. "There's a couple of those fancy-spouting Yankee 'unfortunates' going 'round stirring up all that poor white trash's hangs about here 'n' there along the river by spouting off's how rich folks shouldn't be let stay rich 'n' should ought to be made to share out all they've got with everybody else.''

"There's always somebody, especially Yankee 'unfortunates' spouting off along those lines," Belle said tolerantly and without showing the slightest suggestion of embarrassment, even though she was aware of what was implied by the emphasized word when used in such a fashion. "And, human nature being what it is, they'll *always* find somebody willing to listen.''

"That's not the only thing they're spouting off about, what I've been told," the elderly woman claimed. "They're saying's how all us colored folks should ought to be set free.''

"That's getting said more and more frequently these days," Belle pointed out, but was paying greater attention to what she was told. "Especially by Yankee 'unfortunates' of the kind I figure this pair to be.''

"Then why don't they mind their own business?" Auntie Mattie demanded with all-too obviously sincere indignation. "What my cousin Tildy-Mae from down to the Thatcher place allows her son's told her, I for sure don't want setting free.''

"Would he be the son who ran away?" Belle asked.

"He for sure would," the elderly woman confirmed, and her disapproval was apparent. "Do you mind him? A scrawny, shiftless no-account.''

"I believe I do," the girl answered. "Aunt Margaret said he was a bright boy and took to learning all the schooling she and Momma give to all the children much better than most of them.''

"Oh, he learned all right, for all the good it did him," Auntie Mattie conceded grudgingly. "But that's what getting all this book learning does for young'n's like him. He got to saying he wanted to be free 'n' wound up by getting himself took north on what they call the Underground Railroad, which-ever in the world *that* might be. Only, when he got there, it didn't pan out the way I reckon he'd been led to expect.''

"What went wrong?"

" 'Cording to a letter he sent down to his momma 'n' my Tobias had to read for her seeing's how she can't, up north's not the promised land it's made out to be. He found's how he had to pay for his living place 'n' food, which he'd never had to do afore in his whole life. Top of that, he allows the white working folks up there's allus saying and getting mean over how they reckon us colored folks's go north're taking jobs they should have cheaper than they would. He reckons's how he wished he stayed to home where he didn't get nothing like that.''

''I've heard things aren't anywhere near to what the Yankee 'unfortunates' and their like claim it will be when colored folk get taken north,'' Belle admitted, having read accounts that appeared in newspapers of rioting by white people in northern cities as a protest against the problems caused at their level of society by the arrival of Negroes in search of freedom.

''They for sure ain't 'cording to what that shiftless son of Cousin Tildy-Mae's allows,'' Auntie Mattie affirmed. ''I reckon, happen he could, he'd get that ole Underground Railroad to fetch him right on back home again.'' Then she gave a shrug as if considering that nothing else needed to be said on the subject of her clearly less-than-favorite nephew. ''Anyways, you bear in mind what I told you about staying clear of the piney woods after dark.''

''Don't I *always* bear *everything* you tell me in mind?'' Belle challenged.

''Just so long's how it's something you *wants* to take heed of,'' the elderly woman replied dryly, but once again grew serious. ''Only this time, honey, I want you to do it.''

''I will,'' the girl promised, and as she had rarely seen or heard her former nurse and present mentor behave in such a grave manner, meant what she said.

Even as Belle was making the promise, suddenly sounds originating from outside at ground level came through the window of the room that she had opened on arriving as an aid to keeping it cool.

Going by what she heard and deduced, the girl felt certain that the noises boded nothing good.

Having been sleeping on the front porch as usual, first one and then the other of Belle's bluetick coonhounds, which were trained to hunt solely for raccoon and opossum, began to give the kind of quizzical barking that always greeted people on arrival. However, this comparatively friendly behavior was followed by the roaring growls that precluded the attitude of merely announcing the coming of visitors. She knew such a reaction was unlikely to take place if the followers of the hunt were coming, particularly as Joe Lassiter—who was well known to Bugle and Blue, having bred and trained them as a birthday present for her—would be with them.

Even as the girl exchanged a glance with Auntie Mattie and concluded that the same thoughts were assailing both of them, there was an even greater cause for the alarm both were experiencing.

Two shots sounded, and in the wake of each, one and then the other of the blueticks gave screaming yelps indicative of having sustained a very serious—perhaps even fatal—injury.

Before Belle could reach the window to look out and investigate the reason for her hounds' being shot, there were shouts uttered by numerous masculine voices and the sound of running feet drawing rapidly closer.

Because of what had preceded the latest development, the girl realized the speakers were definitely hostile in their reason for paying the visit.

Next came a crashing that implied that the front entrance to the mansion had been burst open.

The latest extremely worrying noise was followed by a yell of alarm that Belle and Auntie Mattie identified as coming from the latter's husband, who was the butler and majordomo for the Boyd family.

CHAPTER THREE

Kill the Southern Scum!

For all their often-stated hatred of all wealthy slave-owning Southrons, it had never been the intention of Alfred Tollinger and George Barmain to be part of the mob of riffraff they were accompanying through the darkness toward the mansion of Vincent Boyd's Baton Royale plantation.

The pair, who were unwittingly to create a most bitter and deadly efficient foe for the federal armed forces and authorities throughout the years of the War soon to come—and a most loyal servant for the United States when the hostilities were brought to an end—had spent a considerable amount of the money they had been grudgingly supplied with to cover their expenses before leaving Washington, D.C., on entertaining the group they were with in a most unsavory riverside tavern while inveigling them into making an attack on the Boyds' mansion.

Lacking knowledge of the area, Tollinger and Barmain had been directed to the tavern by a less-than-prominent businessman of the local community who had never made known to any of his neighbors his adherence to the political beliefs they practiced. Although they had been assured by him before setting out on their assignment that they would find there men who would be of the greatest use when they reached their objective, he had declined—on the grounds that urgent matters elsewhere demanded his immediate attention—to take any active part in what they intended to do.

However, when the pair arrived, they discovered that the place to which they had been sent offered them the support they would need, even though it was not a kind they would have selected had they been allowed to make a selection. Neither support for the cause being extolled by them—being either completely indifferent or totally opposed to doing anything that might help cause all slaves in the South to be set free—nor the sharing of their "liberal" pretensions over other issues had caused the support to be forthcoming. Rather, with the exception of a trio of exceptionally villainous-looking men from the vicinity who claimed they had a personal grudge to settle and carried along the means to bring it about, the rest were solely motivated by the prospect of acquiring the loot taken from the reputedly very wealthy Boyd family, who owned the property.

Unfortunately for the pair, when the promise of support was given, they had been informed in no uncertain terms that they were to go along. Guessing that a refusal would cause a refusal of the others to participate and might even cause painful repercussions upon them, or at least the loss of the money they had been incautious enough to let be seen while paying for the drinks. Even with those considerations having to be taken into account, they would have lacked the courage to concur if they had not possessed the means to use the dose of cocaine apiece that was needed to give an additional boost to the marijuana cigarettes they smoked as an aid to retaining their self-confidence, which was never strong unless under the influence of narcotics.

For all their having been chosen by men whom it would have been most ill-advised of them to refuse—although compelled would be a more apt description for the means employed to make them go—to carry out the task of arousing anti-Secessionist feelings in Baton Bayou Parish, as the State of Louisiana called what would have been counties elsewhere in the United States, and the surrounding districts, the pair were far from being imposing specimens of manhood likely to inspire support or reliance in their capability of being leaders of men.

Like many of their background and upbringing, the pair had been born into an affluent middle class–middle management stratum of society. From their early childhood, they had been sheltered from anything that might put them into competition with others and imbued with a false sense of personal brilliance capable of taking them to the top of whatever they might deign to attempt. Having met while attending a college already becoming noted for its emphasis upon "liberal" rather than purely educational instruction, they had formed the kind of close relationship that had led Martha Jonias to refer to them as "unfortunates" after the fashion of the day. On graduating, they had quickly discovered themselves unable to obtain the sort of lucrative employment they had felt was high enough to meet their lofty ideas of their respective worth. Instead of seeking something more in keeping with their abilities, if such could have been found, they had drifted into the fringes of the entertainment industry without achieving any greater success. However, this had led them into active participation in the policies advocated by others of their ilk. This had led to them being sent upon a mission to Louisiana that, sensing it might entail taking risks and put them in danger, they would have preferred to avoid.

While costly when new, the three-piece dark-colored suits of the latest Eastern mode, white shirts with celluloid collars, and Hersome gaiter boots worn by Tollinger and Barmain were now grubby and unkempt—more through neglect than because of wear under harsh conditions.

Sporting a derby hat no more clean than his person and the rest of his attire, Tollinger was about six feet tall and skinny in build. Although he believed he possessed great charm, there was an air of ordinariness about him that did nothing to assist his aims to reach great heights with as little effort on his part as possible. He had a gaunt, sallow face with hollow cheeks and thick, sneering lips, giving an added petulance to his large mouth, and his sunken eyes did nothing to lessen the expression.

Having on a flat cap of a style rarely seen anywhere near the Mississippi River and hardly ever west of it, Barmain had a porcine cast of features only a fond mother would have called good-looking. Nor were they improved by his having a drooping straggly black walrus mustache and unkempt greasy long hair. Some three inches shorter than his companion, he had a portly and obviously flabby build that caused him to perspire for the slightest reason. This left him permanently with a stale stench that, although he regarded it as giving him a oneness with the "little people" for whom he professed great concern over the way they were downtrodden by the higher levels of society—while always speaking of them when in the presence of his own kind—was likely to be considered unpleasant to the nostrils of anybody with a delicate stomach.

Despite having been brought to a state of drunkenness in which they were willing to engage in the enterprise proposed by the two Easterners, having covered the distance on foot from the tavern to their destination, all of the riffraff had sobered sufficiently by the time they reached the front gates of the grounds around the mansion to move quietly along the gravel-covered path toward the front of the large and well-lit main building in the hope of taking their intended victims completely by surprise.

Before the hoped-for surprise could be achieved, the two bluetick coonhounds had detected and given notice of the men's coming. To make matters worse, the aggression being shown by the two large and obviously fierce animals after having started to bark warned they would not be frightened away with any means quiet enough to avoid detection by the occupants. Before the attack could be put into effect, instead of trying to find quieter means, a couple of hard cases ended the threat by shooting the approaching hounds with their pistols.

"Come on, men!" Tollinger yelled, his New England accent high-pitched by the excitement induced from having taken, for the second time that night, what a later generation would call a "fix" by "mainlining" under the pretense of answering the call of nature in the bushes shortly before the mansion came into view. "Unless Boyd's come back from hunting, there'll only be his wife and daughter at home."

"And their niggers won't lift a hand to help them," Barmain supplemented, his voice having a similar accent and sounding even less masculine. Also "high" as a result of duplicating his close friend's action after using a similar excuse, he continued in a wild scream, "Kill the Southern scum!"

Having made the comments and exhortation, each drawing the Smith & Wesson No. 1 First Model revolvers with which he was supplied before leaving for Louisiana, the pair started toward the house at a run. If they had had greater experience than was obtained from the limited acquaintance they had had with such devices, they would have been less confident in the guns as a means of offense or defense. Despite the rimfire cartridges being only .22 in caliber, they were impressed by the knowledge that each had no fewer than seven shots avail-

able before there would be any need to reload and doing so
was a far simpler, more rapid, process than when handling a
percussion-fired, generally six-shot revolver. Without being
aware of the disadvantages from their enforced type of armament, having no great amount of courage even when under
the influence of the narcotics, they controlled the rate of their
advance to ensure that there were several of the hard cases
ahead of them.

Passing the dead hounds, the leading men—a burly pair
armed with Colt Model of 1848 Dragoon revolvers—lowered
their shoulders to charge at the front door. Although this
gained the access that was required, it had not been necessary.
Vincent Boyd never kept the front entrance to his home
locked. Nor, until that moment, had their ever been any need
for him to do so. Crossing the threshold, they were confronted
by a clearly startled small, chubby, and immaculately attired
Negro. Before Tobias Jonias could do more than give the cry
of alarm that was heard by his wife and Belle Boyd upstairs,
he was sent sprawling unconscious to the floor by a blow from
the barrel of the heavy revolver in the hand of the taller of the
leading intruders.

Bellowing in delight at having obtained access to the premises with such ease, the other two "liberals" and remaining
hard cases swarmed after the first pair. While Tollinger and
Barmain were accompanied by some of them in following their
inadvertent leaders up the wide stairs leading to the upper floor
of the building, the rest scattered through the rooms on the
ground floor in search of loot to plunder.

* * *

Thankful for having loaded the pair of Manton dueling pistols before going to take the bath, as she had occasionally
added small sums by betting on her ability to use them with
skill to the satisfactory allowance received weekly from her
father—the winning being more important and enjoyable than
the actual money involved—Belle Boyd cocked back each
hammer on taking them in turn from their box without waiting
to discover what threat might be posed by the commotion
downstairs. Holding them ready for use, she darted across the
room and went through its door.

On entering the passage, Belle saw that she was not a moment too soon.

Already the girl's mother and father, the former looking like an older version of herself, were coming from their quarters. Each was carrying a Colt revolver, supplemented by a cavalry saber in the case of Vincent Boyd, and she knew they were as capable as herself of using the weapons. This was proved by her father turning and firing to send a bullet into the torso of the first ruffianly-looking man to reach the head of the stairs from the ground floor. However, there were too many others closely following for Boyd to deal with them all unaided. Even as Belle was raising and firing the pistol in her right hand, she saw her mother shoot at the next of the attackers.

Unfortunately, Electra Boyd and Belle had inadvertently selected the same target. Struck in the head and chest by the two bullets, the second of the men who had forced the entrance into the mansion was twirled around and dropped without being allowed to use his own weapon. While the girl was changing her pistols, being a better shot with her right hand, she saw the men she suspected as being the "unfortunates" mentioned by Auntie Mattie when delivering the warning about the possible danger of going hunting alone in the woods at night. Without knowing their identity, she concluded that they were posing a most dangerous threat to her parents.

Somehow having been pushed into the forefront of the mob while ascending the stairs, Tollinger and Barmain were the next to arrive on the second floor. They were most alarmed when they discovered that the women they had believed would be the sole white occupants of the mansion were accompanied by its owner. What was more, as was proved by the fate of the first pair to confront Boyd, his wife, and the slender, skimpily clad girl who was obviously their daughter, each of them was proving to be most competent in handling the weapons they were holding.

Fright close to a sensation of numbing terror erupted through both of the "liberals" simultaneously when a full appreciation of their danger struck home. However, the realization provoked each to respond with greater alacrity than would have been the case if granted time to think. Bringing up the

Smith & Wesson revolvers in the kind of double-handed way they had discovered on the few occasions when they were carrying out practice, they sighted and began to shoot as fast as they could squeeze the trigger to operate the double-action mechanism. By chance rather than any kind of deliberate intent, they selected different marks at which to fire.

Firing from such a close range, and aided by the light weight and far-from-potent recoil kick of their weapons, Tollinger and Barmain were able to make hit after hit upon their inadvertently chosen victims. The former sent each bullet into the body of Electra Boyd and the latter directed his attention to seeking the same general target on her husband. Even with the puny powder load and diminutive .22-caliber loads that were all the early example of metal cartridge-handling weapons could handle, the cumulative effect of seven pieces of lead driving into the torso in rapid succession was too great for either recipient to be able to fend it off.

Although Boyd managed to discharge his Colt Model of 1848 Dragoon revolver, its .44-caliber ball went over Barmain's head and he followed his wife, her Model of 1849 Pocket Pistol—also a revolver despite its given name—remaining unfired, in going down. Seeing what had befallen her parents, a scream that seemed closer to animal than human burst from Belle. However, she did not restrict herself to just the vocal response. Letting the discharged pistol drop, she sent her liberated left hand to join the right on the butt of its mate to adopt the same kind of shooting posture the "liberals" were using and sighted on the head of the one who had fired at her mother.

Barmain should have died at that moment.

However, just as Belle completed the required pressure on the set-trigger of the excellently made British pistol and its hammer snapped downward toward the waiting percussion cap that would have set off the powder in the chamber, impelled by a desire to be first to select booty, the foremost of the other men jostled him aside. Through the swirling white smoke of the exploded charge, the girl saw him struck in the shoulder by the bullet she had dispatched with the intention of avenging the attack upon her mother.

Alarmed by what he realized had been a very close escape

from injury or perhaps even death, the shorter of the "liberals" allowed the rest of the hard cases to go by. Being made aware by the repeated metallic click's of the descending hammer, instead of detonations, which were sounding that his revolver was empty, Tollinger behaved in the same fashion. Then, exchanging glances as they mutually—and without the need for discussion—concluded that the resistance being put up was much greater than they had anticipated and could be reaching an unacceptably dangerous level, the pair swung around to return hurriedly to the ground floor and left the building.

Added to the realization that the commotion might be heard by the Boyds' neighbors and bring armed assistance, knowing how competent it was certain to be, what Tollinger and Barmain saw happening closer at hand was sufficient to send them scurrying along the gravel path toward the front entrance of the property as fast as their legs—given the impulsion caused by fear of the consequences—could carry them. From the continued sounds of conflict that followed them, they realized that the fighting inside the building was still going on and their only desire was to put as much distance as possible at the greatest speed they could muster between themselves and what they had caused to happen.

Having no doubt what their fate would be if they were captured, the pair also concluded that—regardless of their orders or how others engaged elsewhere in the South upon the same mission might be faring—they would make all haste in returning to the safety of an area with stout pro-Northern sympathies.

Having the small-minded, vindictive, and untrustworthy natures of their kind, the pair decided to take revenge upon the local "liberal" businessman they held responsible for their predicament. Confident there was no way in which he could retaliate, as he did not even know that the names they were using were assumed for the assignment, they would betray him to the authorities when clear of the immediate danger area. However, having similar characteristics in his makeup, the intended victim, on hearing news of what happened, also fled to security from capture presented by settling in antislavery-committed territory.

CHAPTER FOUR

Our Menfolks're On Their Way

With the load from the second Manton dueling pistol discharged, Belle Boyd did not waste as much as a second by indulging in futile mental recriminations, despite experiencing a surge of anger over the failure to hit her intended target even though she was aware that her aim was not at fault. Allowing the English-made weapon to fall alongside its earlier-fired and discarded mate, watching more of the invaders coming her way and realizing she must acquire the means to deal with whatever evil they might contemplate, she turned and darted back toward the door of her suite. Seeing her coming, having been on the point of following her into the passage, Martha Jonias drew back with an alacrity that seemed out of place for one of such an age and bulk.

"Please get the Colt from my bedside table!" the girl said as she went by the elderly Negress, the lessons she had received in good manners causing her to employ the first word despite the extreme urgency of the situation.

Without waiting to reply, Auntie Mattie showed a similar speed when getting out of the girl's way by closing the door before going to carry out the request. However, knowing there was no way in which it could be secured—locks and bolts never having been considered necessary for rooms inside the mansion of Baton Royale plantation—she immediately and just as swiftly went to carry out the instructions she was given. Paying no further attention to her former nurse and now mentor, Belle hurried toward the fireplace of the sitting room.

Reaching up, the girl lifted the outer of the two swords from where it hung across its almost identical mate below the fencing mask. Giving it a swishing motion as if limbering up to engage in a practice bout, then hearing a crash and guessing at its cause, she turned in the direction from which she had come. As she guessed had happened, one of the men, being unaware of the rules that prevailed in her home where such

things were concerned, had charged into and burst open the
door. Because the entrance to the sitting room had been effected far more easily than he anticipated, he staggered out of
control across the threshold. However, two more of the raiding
party were close on his heels.

Much to her annoyance, Belle saw that none of the men
were the pair she had seen shoot down her parents. However,
she felt some slight relief from observing that they were not
carrying firearms. Because each held a knife of sizable dimensions, she concluded on that account that they were far from
being innocuous. Passing his still-staggering companion, the
first of the pair darted toward her. Despite seeing the sword
she was grasping, he felt sure he had nothing to fear from the
skimpily attired and curvaceously slender girl regardless of the
expression of grim determination and deadly loathing on her
beautiful face.

The hard case soon discovered how wrong his conclusion
had been.

Responding as her training at fencing taught her, Belle went
to meet her would-be assailant with the swift and competent
precision of one well-versed in such matters, despite putting
the knowledge to use in earnest for the first time. Going into
a close-to-perfect classical lunge, she sent the shining blade of
her weapon driving toward the man. Showing an appreciation
of his peril and possessing sufficient control over his movements to be able to take evasive action, he made a rapid withdrawal that carried him beyond the range of the attack, even
though doing so caused him to run up against the man who
had effected the entrance.

Following up the thwarted attack, the girl prepared to make
the best possible use of the qualities that made the *épée de
combat* she was holding such an effective weapon. Unlike a
foil, which could only be employed to make a lunging thrust
with the point, the edges of its blade were sharpened so as to
permit cutting and slashing after the fashion of the heavier
saber. It was this kind of tactic she elected to put into practice.
However, while commencing to deliver the cut at the head she
was contemplating—despite the rage she was still experiencing
over the shooting of her parents—her instincts and upbringing
revolted against inflicting an injury that would almost certainly

cause the death of another human being. Therefore, at the last moment she changed her target. Instead of slashing into the man's throat, the blade laid open his right cheek in a way that would scar him for life.

Watching the devastating speed and obvious competence with which Belle was making the attack, the third of the men decided against taking her on with the knife he held. Despite the length of its blade, it was considerably shorter than the sword she was wielding so effectively. With that thought in mind, he saw a means of avoiding the need to do so. What was more, he considered that he was suitably equipped by virtue of his birth and upbringing to make the most of the opportunity. A French Creole from a moderately wealthy family who had turned to a life of crime after having been disowned by his father for being caught cheating at cards, he had received instruction in fencing while growing up. Although he had not kept up the practice after fleeing from the wrath of the men he had cheated, he was confident that he could still use the more suitable weapon he had noticed on entering the room.

Transferring the knife into his left hand, the Creole darted over to reach with the right for the second épée on the wall.

Hoping to achieve surprise, as he had no liking for the prospect of having to engage in serious combat with one who was such an obviously capable antagonist regardless of her sex, the Creole swung around with it in his grasp. Much to his relief, as he had been made aware of how effectively she could wield the weapon, he found that the girl had turned her attention to the man who had forced the entry for them. Confident he would be able to make the attack before being detected, he advanced and went into a lunge, as he had been taught. In his haste, he made it from slightly farther away than he intended.

However, with his intended victim's attention being distracted, the Creole felt sure he would still achieve his purpose.

Having recovered his equilibrium and thrust the wounded man aside, the hard case who had gained admittance to the room with an unneeded charge at the door found himself able to tackle the beautiful girl. On the point of lunging at her, he heard a feminine bellow redolent of a close-to-bestial rage and swung his gaze toward its source. Although he realized that there was a potentially grave danger threatening from that direction, he reacted too slowly to prevent it from happening.

Returning with the five-shot ivory-handled Colt Little Dragoon Pocket Pistol revolver that Belle kept loaded and capped in the drawer of her bedside table, Auntie Mattie, never having fired any kind of weapon, made no attempt to use it. Instead, letting it fall from her grasp, she rushed forward while emitting the roar that drew the attention of the burly man her way. Before his never-swift wits could cope with the unexpected turn of events, although he read the menace in the massive old Negress's demeanor, he felt his throat grasped by a hand with a grip like a closing bear trap.

Having the waist band of his trousers seized at the same moment that the other hold was applied to inflict a choking that further numbed his already bewildered senses, the man felt himself being propelled backward with a force he would have been hard-pressed to resist even if the grip were not being applied so vigorously. Just as he was trying to halt, he found he was being subjected to a surging thrust that sent him against the window. Going through to the sound of shattering glass, a wail of alarm burst from him as he was falling to crash on the ground. Unable to halt before, Auntie Mattie contrived to do so by placing her palms on the wall alongside the ruined casement. Seeing and hearing certain happenings that were taking place below, she swung around with the intention of alerting Belle to them.

Although the Creole made the lunge as he had intended, he found that it failed to achieve the desired effect. On coming into contact with the left biceps of the girl as she started to turn his way, instead of her back as he had intended—satisfied that being struck there would leave her sufficiently incapacitated for him to take the retaliatory measures his lecherous disposition was planning to extract—the anticipated penetration failed to materialize. Instead of the point sinking into flesh, the blade began to bend upward in a graceful curve.

The error made by the girl's latest would-be attacker was one of ignorance.

Although coming from the same maker as the épée de combat and matching its dimensions exactly, the sword taken from the wall appeared identical only in some respects to the one in Belle's hand. In fact, although the Creole failed to take the matter into account when grabbing it from the wall, it had two vitally important differences in its construction. Designed for use at fencing practice only, in the interests of avoiding the chance of injury to an opponent, the edges of the blade were not sharpened and the tip had been fitted with a protective metal "button" intended to prevent its penetrating when making a "hit" at the conclusion of a successful lunge. Therefore, its employment as a means of defense and attack was far from being as dangerous as was the case with the weapon—rather than a sporting device—she was holding.

Feeling the pain as the contact by the blade of the practice épée came, the girl reacted with speed. Coming around, she once more struck back with what started as a cut to the head and, still being under the influence of her instinctive objection to doing something that could possibly take the life of another human being, she lowered her point of aim to lay open the Creole's right upper arm to the bone. The pain and severing of the biceps caused him to drop both the knife and the ineffective sword with which he had hoped to counter the épée de combat she was using so effectively.

However, despite having disposed of her assailant and seeing that Auntie Mattie had coped with an even greater severity while removing the other threat, the girl discovered that she could not account herself safe from further danger.

Nevertheless, Belle was given an intimation that help might be forthcoming.

"Our menfolks're on their way, gal!" Auntie Mattie yelled, turning from the window after having seen the figures armed with a variety of improvised weapons who were approaching rapidly from the living quarters allocated to them. A glance farther away allowed her to deliver a further piece of information, which she regarded as being of equal importance if she should be correct in what was portended by it. "And there's riders a-coming fast!"

Although gratified by the news given by the Negress, as she knew the loyalty all their workforce showed toward her family and deduced that the approaching horsemen would be the rest of the hunting party returning from assisting Joe Lassiter in attending to the muck ponies they had ridden, and knowing they would all be armed even though no weapons were carried while going out for the evening's sport, the girl realized that the peril she and Auntie Mattie were facing was not yet at an end. The two men she had wounded were put out of action, or at least sufficiently incapacitated to be rendered close to innocuous until recovering from the injuries sustained, but she saw yet another of the attackers coming through the door. What was more, unlike his three predecessors, he was carrying a cocked muzzle-loading pistol in his right hand.

Skidding to a halt, the man brought the heavy-caliber firearm into a shoulder-height alignment upon the girl.

Before the latest intruder could squeeze the trigger of his weapon, Auntie Mattie made her presence known in the same way she had done previously. Hearing the awesome roar and looking at its source, the man was not led into a sense of false security by discovering it was emanating from an elderly woman—and a Negress, at that. Deducing the very real threat she was posing to himself, while the girl at whom he was aiming stood a greater distance away, he swung the pistol around and completed the pressure already commenced. With a deep coughing roar, the charge was detonated and the heavy ball of lead left the muzzle to plow into Auntie Mattie's ample torso. Not even her massive bulk could offset the effect of the impact. Giving a cry of pain, she had her advance turned into an involuntary retreat that ended with her sprawling supine on the floor.

Seeing what had happened to the elderly woman, Belle was filled with a desire to take revenge upon the man responsible. However, the instincts that came from being the product of a race of fighters on both sides of her family warned that attempting to do so while armed only with the épée would be ill-advised. She had not noticed that the pistol had only a single barrel and so was useless as a firearm until reloaded. What she did know was that there were other would-be attackers who might soon be arriving and some more effective means than cold steel would be required if she was to defend herself and Auntie Mattie from them.

Fortunately, Belle thought, the means she required was close at hand.

Allowing the épée to fall from her grasp, Belle went in a rolling dive that took her to where the Negress had dropped her Colt. Closing her right hand around the ivory butt, which had never felt so comforting as it did at that moment, she came to her knees. With her left hand joining its mate, she completed the move on her knees facing the man and started to raise the short-barreled weapon. The move was as smoothly accomplished as if it had been practiced a great many times until a peak of perfection was achieved, instead of being made for the first time and only by instinctive reflexes. However, she was prevented from bringing it to the kind of conclusion she desired.

Seeing the response being made by Belle and hearing yells accompanied by other significant sounds from outside the room, the man was all too aware of how precarious his situation had become. Letting out a snarl of rage, his instincts warning that she possessed sufficient knowledge to be able to shoot with enough accuracy to put his life at risk, he hurled the empty pistol at her with the intention of distracting her aim before she could open fire. Having done so, he ran to the shattered window and, springing through, alighted on the feebly moving body of his predecessor to leave—albeit involuntarily—by that route. Ignoring the moan of agony that greeted his arrival, he started to run across the grounds as swiftly as his legs would carry him.

Chance rather than a skilled aim caused the pistol to achieve a result the man would have been pleased to witness.

Caught on the side of the head by the butt of the approaching weapon before she could deflect it, Belle was toppled sideways; She was stunned by the impact, and blackness descended upon her.

CHAPTER FIVE

I'm Going to See Both of Them Dead!

Shortly after Belle Boyd was rendered unconscious by the pistol thrown at her, two of the men who had been on the fox hunt earlier in the evening and a pair of Negroes clad in attire suggesting that they were field hands rather than members of the mansion's domestic staff dashed into the room.

Already from below the sounds of fighting had died away from the ground floor, although there were other indications that activity of a hostile nature was continuing in the grounds.

Furthermore, originating from somewhere on the ground floor, there were other noises suggesting that efforts were being made to put out the fires that had been started in various parts of the mansion. These had been started, using kerosene, by the members of the mob holding a grudge against the owner of Baton Royale plantation for his part in curtailing some of their unsavory activities. Therefore, although Belle and the others on the upper floor were unaware of the problem, because of the highly inflammable nature of much of their surroundings as well as the fluid employed to set each blaze going and the primitive means that were being employed in an attempt to douse the resulting blazes, the men fighting the fires were finding great difficulty in achieving anything against the ever-growing flames.

Realizing the danger posed by the spreading conflagration, the quartet had come to the second floor to give whatever succor was needed to its occupants and ensure that there were no more of the attackers about. It had only needed a quick examination to inform them that there was nothing anybody could do for the owner and his wife. However, as neither had put in an appearance down below, they had surmised that the daughter of the house and possibly her former maid were upstairs. It had been the biggest of the Negroes who guessed where the women could be found.

"Quickly!" snapped Phillipe Front de Boeuf,[1] the young white man in the lead. Dressed as he had been during the hunt, although lacking the most undesirable qualities some of his family had had and one at least still possessed, he had the size and bulk for which most members his family had long been renowned.[1a] "Get them downstairs and outside."

"You 'tend to my li'l lamb first!" Mattie Jonias croaked, trying to force herself up from a kneeling position while still keeping her right hand clasped to the wound in the right side of her torso just below her massive bosom.

"We'll see to you *both*!" Front de Boeuf asserted. He was a medical student and knew enough about such injuries as the old Negress had sustained to appreciate the danger of what must be done, but he was aware there was no other choice if she was to be saved from the flames. "Danny, help get Belle downstairs. We'll see to Auntie Mattie." His eyes went to the woman and he continued in a gentle voice, "It's going to hurt, but we have to carry you out of here."

"Not 'til my li'l lamb's safe away!" Auntie Mattie denied heatedly and weakly, trying to fend off the approaching men with her hands. "You get to toting her off downstairs, Sammy-well!"

"I can do it easier'n the two of us, boss," stated the shorter of the Negroes, which did not make him small or feeble in build.

"Very well," assented the young white man who had almost landed on the girl when they took the fall with their

[1] *Sir Reginald Front de Boeuf, master of Torquilstoen Castle in medieval England, was an early example of more unsavory members of the family. See* IVANHOE *by Sir Walter Scott.*

[1a] *Two descendants of Sir Reginald who inherited his worst traits were Jessica and her only son, Trudeau Front de Boeuf. To antagonize the rest of the family, she always used the surname instead of that of the man she married. Incidents involving their criminal activities are recorded in* CUT ONE, THEY ALL BLEED; *Part Three, "Responsibility to Kinfolks,"* OLE DEVIL'S HANDS AND FEET; *and Part Four, "The Penalty of False Arrest,"* MARK COUNTER'S KIN.

[1b] *Mark Counter inherited the physique but not the objectionable traits from the maternal side of his bloodline. Information regarding his family background and special qualifications is given in the* Floating Outfit *series.*

horses in the woodland. "I'll fetch along these swords and pistols. I know how much Belle cared for them."

"Get some clothes for her from the bedroom closet, sir!" Auntie Mattie said, making the words more of a demand than a request. "They'll be a whole heap more use right now than them fool weapons of her'n regardless of how she would insist on playing with 'em."

"Yes, ma'am," the young Southron answered, instinctively speaking with the politeness he would have employed if it had been his own colored "mammy" addressing him. "I'll 'tend to it!"

Refusing to let the two big men lift her until she had seen the girl being borne through the door in the arms of "Sammywell" and her instructions regarding the collection of garments being obeyed, the elderly Negress submitted to being removed as soon as she was satisfied that all was being done as she wanted it. Although the of necessity swift way in which she was being carried by the shoulders and upper thighs between the equally massive and well-muscled pair caused her great pain, she did not allow more than the occasional extra-heavy exhalation of breath to give an indication of her suffering. There was, she realized, a pressing need for haste. Already the flames were gaining to such an extent that she realized there would be little saved of the mansion that had been her home for a great many years. She wondered how the girl she had done so much to raise—and secretly admired for qualities that were not a normal requisite of the wealthy Southron maiden—would react when she learned what had happened.

Although some more of the men tried to come to the floor and fetch down the bodies of Electra and Vincent Boyd, the ferocity of the conflagration defeated them. In fact, the staircase was already beginning to quiver with an increasing violence as the still-unconscious girl and injured Negress were being carried down. The latter had only just arrived on the comparative safety of the ground floor when flames began to lick upward to consume the steps; a few seconds later, the staircase collapsed, cutting off access to the upper portion of the building from that direction. Having stopped to gather up Belle's weapon in addition to the clothing he had grabbed at random—including some of the masculine attire and the boots she had worn for the hunt—Front de Boeuf was the last to descend, and it was only by taking a flying leap before reaching the final six or so feet that he was able to escape being trapped by the disintegration of what had been part of the pride of Baton Royale's fixtures.

Driven backward by the heat and fumes, with the exception of the men who had come in the hope of effecting a rescue, all who were driven from the mansion by the flames stood in silence as they watched impotently the destruction of what had been a fine and happy home. While Front de Boeuf was putting his medical training to use in what was to prove a successful bid to keep Auntie Mattie alive until a more experienced local practitioner of the healing arts could arrive, the rest expressed their feelings in whatever way their temperaments called for. Their vocal efforts were accompanied by the wailing of the Negresses who had followed their menfolk when it became apparent that an attack upon the mansion was taking place and, some of them at least, had played a not-ineffective part in helping to rout the mob.

Furthermore, it was only with some difficulty that the furious women were restrained from dealing in a most painful manner with the three men who had failed to make good an escape. Not that, in view of the less-than-gentle way they were treated to extract information that would be of help to the local peace officers when investigating the cause of the attack, they were inclined to consider the change of sex where their interrogators was concerned to have been noticeably more beneficial. Regardless of coming from well-to-do families and having been raised with a strict respect for the due processes of the law, the young guests on what had turned out to be Vincent Boyd's last hunt had had no qualms over the means employed by Joe Lassiter. Claiming to have Seminole Indian blood, he had applied what he said were methods acquired from that nation of savagely efficient swamp-dwelling and -fighting warriors to procure the answers.

*   *   *

"What happened to Momma and Poppa?" Belle Boyd asked in tones redolent of the grief she was trying to keep in check after she had recovered sufficiently from the blow by the thrown pistol to take notice of her surroundings. She was sitting up with her back resting against a stone wall that she had often rested against while playing on the grounds of the mansion. *"Please* tell me, Reverend Jacob!"

Once safely removed from the burning building, the still-unconscious girl had been carried to a small summer-house that stood unscathed by the attack not far from where her home was being gutted by the fire. On carrying out a quick examination of her injury, before starting to do what he could for Auntie Mattie, Phillipe Front de Boeuf had satisfied himself that she was in no immediate danger. There was a blue-black contusion on the side of her head where the contact with the weapon was made, but the skin had not been cut. Concluding that there was nothing more he could do for her at that moment, he had given instructions to the little Negress who served as her maid to get her into some more adequate attire. Leaving this to be carried out, knowing there was no need for him to remain to supervise the covering of the skimpy undergarments—which he had checked and found to his relief carried bloodstains from her assailants and were not caused by her own having been shed in the fighting—he had returned to devote his full attention to the elderly woman who had insisted that he see to the needs of her "li'l lamb" first.

"I'm sorry to have to tell you this, child," the oldest member of the hunting party replied, his voice brittle with anger and remorse. He was the Reverend Jacob Keith, and as minister of the Episcopalian church at Baton Rouge, he had always been a good friend of the Boyd family. He had known the girl since the day she was born, and in addition to officiating at her christening, had often been a coconspirator with her father where the less-than-conventional aspects of her education were concerned. A sturdy and cheery man in his early fifties, he was respected by his parishioners for his warmth, and the pithy sermons he preached were much admired by the majority of those who heard them. Furthermore, his keenness to indulge in all kinds of hunting and fishing, as well as a tolerance toward drinking hard liquor provided it was done in moderation, except on Sundays or the recognized church holidays, endeared him to the younger male members of his community. However, he had never relished less anything he had carried out in accordance with his duties around the parish than the task he was now facing. "But they were both killed."

"I saw it happen," Belle said in a voice barely louder than a whisper, but in tones redolent of her deep sense of bitterness as she remembered how she had failed to shoot either of the men who had done the killing. Then a shudder she could not restrain ran through her slender yet curvaceous frame and she asked in only a slightly less softly spoken voice, "Where are they now?"

"We had to leave them where they fell," Keith answered just as quietly, and he felt the girl's hands tighten upon his in a grip that made him wince. "I'm sorry, Belle, but there was nothing else we could do. By the time you and Auntie Mattie had been brought down, the stairs were too far gone with the flames for anybody to go up again. There wasn't a shortage of volunteers, black and white, to make a try by the servants' stairs, but I found it was the same there and wouldn't let them take the chance. Knowing them as I did, I felt your mother and father wouldn't have wanted lives lost for them under the circumstances."

"I know that," the girl admitted, and realizing just how tightly she had hold, loosened her grasp on the minister's hands. She looked toward where her home was rapidly being reduced to a blazing ruin and with a shudder braced herself. "Momma and Poppa always loved Baton Royale so much. Somehow I think they would feel more content to know they are still with it even though it's almost gone."

"I think they would, too, although I probably shouldn't come right out and say so," Keith asserted, being opposed to cremation as a prelude to burial in most circumstances. "How do you feel?"

"My head aches, but I'm all right otherwise," Belle replied. Then she let out a gasp and made as if to stand up. "Where's Auntie Mattie?"

"They brought her out safely," the Reverend answered, laying gently restraining hands on the girl's shoulders and feeling the wiry strength he already had cause to know was possessed by her trim body.

"I think I saw her shot," the girl gasped, but felt too weak to get up and look for herself. "In fact, I *know* I did. It happened while she was saving my life."

"She was shot, all right, and is suffering from a bad wound

in the torso," Keith admitted. "But young Front de Boeuf is doing all he can for her, and he's proving surprisingly good at it after the trouble his family had to get him to take up medicine instead of joining the Army or going ranching in Texas with his uncle Winston. Fortunately, Doctor Soames is dining with the Thatchers. They're sure to have heard the disturbance, and the Colonel is sure to come with men to find out what's happened, so he will be able to take over when he arrives."[2]

"How about Poppa Jonias?" Belle wanted to know, fresh thoughts flooding back and causing her to realize that the post of butler was so ably performed by Auntie Mattie's small and always cheerfully efficient husband that he was sure to have been waiting somewhere on the ground floor ready to admit the members of the hunt when they arrived from helping Joe Lassiter attend to the muck ponies they had used.

"He was knocked unconscious by one of them," the minister replied. "But they got him out and he's come 'round. As Mattie can't, some of the other women are taking care of him."

"I hope they are some she approves of," Belle remarked, feeling the need to say something completely inconsequential to relieve her tensed nerves and being all too aware how her former "mammy" and now mentor was very aware of the social distinctions. "I wouldn't *dare* say so to her face, but Auntie Mattie has always struck me as being something of a snob."

"And you're well advised *not* to say so, my girl, for shame," Keith asserted, knowing the reasons for the remark and wanting to help bring about the desired result.

Before any more could be said, Lassiter and one of the party who had ridden his muck ponies in the hunt came up dragging a bedraggled, bloodied, and obviously very frightened man between them.

"This son of a bit—!" the huntsman began, then brought the words to a halt as he realized he was speaking in an inappropriate fashion under the prevailing conditions, regardless

[2] *Although Winston Front de Boeuf was a successful rancher, he did not remain based in Texas; see* THE CODE OF DUSTY FOG.

of his own feeling on the subject. "Sorry, Be—Miss Boyd, Reverend. This stinking river-rat just can't *wait* to start answering questions."

"Don't let them—!" the clearly terrified and already suffering captive yelled, looking at the minister.

"I'd say that all depends on *you*," Keith answered with no sign of sympathy. "I want to hear everything that will help the law get the rest of you scum."

"So do I," Belle declared, and she no longer looked like the young and friendly girl whom the minister had known from the day of her birth. Rather, she was even more cold and pitiless in the way she appeared than Lassiter, for all his Seminole blood. "Especially about the two men who killed my parents. Because I'm going to see both of them dead!"

"No, Belle," the minister said quietly, despite guessing that he was speaking in vain. He also realized that it was one of the very few times he had thought of the girl in terms of her sex. "That's no work for *you*."

"Yes it *is*, Reverend Jacob," the girl contradicted with vehemence. "Poppa always wanted to have a son and couldn't, so he trained me to take that place. Now it is up to me to be the son he always wanted, and that is what I intend to do."

At that moment, Belle Boyd was set upon the path that would gain her the sobriquet Rebel Spy.

CHAPTER SIX

You've Come to the *Wrong* Place

"Y ou have no financial worries, Belle," Counsellor
Seamus O'Connel said in his usual dryly legal tones,
which had only the slightest trace of his Irish origins,
looking at the slender girl clad in the formal attire of mourning
who was seated at his desk. Having been on terms of close
friendship with her family for a great many years, he was
finding difficulty keeping up a pose of coldly businesslike purpose in his demeanor. "I have all the information from the
bank and your people have been through the ruins of Baton
Royale Manor. They've found all your mother's and your jewelry. Some of the settings are damaged, but the actual stones
have come through unscathed."

Three days had elapsed since the attack upon Belle Boyd's
home had caused the death of her parents.

Alarmed by the reports he was given about the disturbance,
Colonel Dennis T. Thatcher had come from his home as fast
as his horse could carry him. He had been accompanied by
his male dinner guests, including Doctor Calvin Soames and
a couple of politicians involved in the ever-worsening dispute
that was growing over whether Louisiana should join the other
Southern states in announcing secession from the Union. Vincent Boyd would have been attending, but he had had the fox
hunt planned before learning it was to take place and suspected
there might be no more for some time, since all the younger
men were to enroll in the Army of the Confederate States as
soon as word came that hostilities were commenced.

Being in favor of secession and knowing how useful they
would be in that capacity, also how such a pleasurable experience was certain to be curtailed once they entered the service,
the Colonel had agreed that the outing must take place as arranged and excused his old friend from the need to attend on
that account. He and the men accompanying him were distressed to discover that they had arrived too late to supply the

intended succor. However, the doctor had examined Mattie Jonias and stated his approval of the way in which Phillipe Front de Boeuf had dealt with the treatment of her wound and announced, to Belle's relief, that she was already on the road to recovery.

For her part, relieved by the good news about the elderly Negress who was now the closest person to her in the world, the girl had been taken to the Thatcher family's mansion and instructed by its owner and his wife, Margaret, to consider it her home for as long as she wished to remain. Although grateful for the kindness and hospitality she received, she had not allowed herself to be swayed from her determination to seek revenge against the two men she held most responsible for everything that happened to Baton Royale Manor, and especially the murder of her parents. What was more, every member of the foxhunting expedition in which she and her father had engaged offered his services in any way they might be needed. They had stated that they would be willing to forgo joining the regiments to which they were already assigned until having helped her achieve her vengeance regardless of whether or not they were given official sanction to do so, but she had refused to let them chance ruining their careers by taking such a course in her behalf.

Supplied with names of the other participants—and in some cases the most likely places to look—by the three captives taken during the fighting at the mansion—without inquiring too closely into how the information was obtained even though it was all too apparent that this had not been supplied on a voluntary basis—the sheriff of Baton Rouge Parish was doing everything he could to bring the rest of the mob to justice. Several were caught and stood trial for their participation, while others were killed resisting arrest. However, the two who mattered most to Belle had succeeded in making good their escape. What was more, by having fled to the North according to all he learned, they were considered by the peace officer as being beyond his or any other Southern jurisdiction.

Consumed by her bitter hatred of the pair she had seen kill her mother and father though she was, but refusing to let it cloud her judgment to a point where she could not think properly about the enormity of the task she was setting herself, the

girl had had most useful allies in her quest. Under the orders of Mattie and Tobias Jonias, both of whom wielded considerable power over them—the former having acquired a
reputation for being a "conjure woman" of considerable potency—the colored people from the plantation and surrounding
area had given assistance that provided information she could
not have obtained through any other source. It was from them
that Belle learned the only names by which she would ever
know the two Yankee "unfortunates," as Auntie Mattie had
referred to Alfred Tollinger and George Barmain. However,
even the Negroes could not discover exactly where the pair
had gone once fleeing from the mansion. That had not lessened
Belle's resolve to find and, if justice could not be achieved in
any other way, kill them herself.

The girl did not delude herself by thinking that the task to
which she was committed would be simple or easy to bring to
the required conclusion. Therefore, after having had Reverend
Keith perform the funeral rights at the ruins of her home on
the morning after the attack, she had begun to think over the
means by which her purpose might be achieved. Typical of
the way she had been raised to think, her first priority had
been to take care of the welfare of the family's loyal and
devoted workforce.

Unlike what a later generation would try to insist was the
only way all Negroes thought about their owners, every one
of them had been distressed by what had happened and eager
to see the murders of their master and mistress avenged. They
also asked no more than they be allowed to remain in their
comfortable homes and help with the rebuilding of the manor
by continuing to carry out whatever their work might be. Being
determined to do all she could for them, Belle had given the
instructions to her family's attorney that resulted in the meeting now taking place at his office.

"Then Baton Royale can continue to be run?" Belle inquired.

"Of course," O'Connel confirmed. "Of course, you will
have to take a man beyond the age for military service to act
as your supervisor, as I don't doubt war will break out against
the Yankees any day now, if it hasn't started already."

"I'm going to ask Uncle Dennis to do so in my absence,"

the girl declared, having always thought of Colonel Thatcher—and his wife, for that matter—in such a fashion despite there being no actual family connections between them. "I'll be staying with him and Aunt Margaret until I leave."

"Yes," the attorney said, nodding in approval. "I feel you're wise to go away for a while and try to put what's happened out of your mind. When will you go and where, so I can keep in touch with you over anything that should develop?"

"I don't know for sure where I'll be going," Belle admitted truthfully. "And I won't be leaving until I've attended to a few things which I won't be able to do wherever I have to go. But, when the time comes, I want Uncle Dennis to have my power of attorney to act completely in my behalf for as long as I am away."

"That's very wise of you," O'Connel praised. "In fact, it is what I would have advised myself."

"I'll also want to have the means to have access to whatever money I might need while I'm gone."

"That can easily enough be arranged through the bank."

"Will you attend to it for me as quickly as possible, please?"

"That's one of the things I'm here for, my dear," the attorney declared, looking at the girl in a speculative fashion and noticing that there was something in addition to an understandably deep grief over the death of her parents in her demeanor, although he was unable to decide exactly what it might be for all of his well-developed judgment of human nature in general and knowledge of her personality in particular. "And you can't tell me definitely where you're planning to go, or how long it will be before you come back?"

"No," Belle admitted quietly, yet her grim sense of purpose and determination to see it through was just discernible to the man across the desk from her. Her tone did not change as she continued, "I've no idea where I may have to go, nor how long it will take me to do what I have to do."

*　*　*

Thinking of the way in which she would soon be dressed, Belle Boyd was pleased that Mattie Tobias was still not suf-

ficiently recovered to have witnessed the choice she had made
for the attire she considered was best suited for the visit she
was intending to carry out. She was sure that neither the garb
she had selected nor the man she was going to see would have
met with the massive elderly Negress's approval. However,
she considered that Captain Anatol de-Farge could be of vital
use to her purpose if she could persuade him to do as she
wished.

Out of consideration for what she hoped to achieve by the
visit she was about to make, the girl felt she was fortunate that
the young man assigned to the task by Auntie Mattie had included the garments—including the black riding boots she
prized so highly for their comfortable fit and the freedom of
movement they permitted—she had worn during the fox hunt
with the clothing he fetched from her bedroom. It was equally
fortuitous that he had also fetched her *épée de combat* and
brace of Manton dueling pistols, although he had not had time
to collect the Colt revolver, even if he had noticed it lying
where it was dropped by Auntie Mattie. She had already replaced it with one of the same model, but was not taking it
with her.

As something of Belle's less-than-conventional upbringing
was well known to all the staff of the Thatcher mansion, while
making it plain that he did not approve of such a flouting of
accepted standards of behavior, the groom who had made
ready the horse from Baton Royale that she was going to use
had made no comment when being told she did not want it to
be fitted with a sidesaddle which to his way of thinking was
the only style a young woman of quality should use. Watching
her riding away, he grudgingly conceded that—despite having
been compelled to adopt the modified version caused by the
rig she selected lacking the support for the left leg offered by
the only acceptable type of female riding gear—she was contriving to handle the spirited horse without any noticeable difficulty. He also wondered why she had asked him to attach
the sword and brace of pistols, which were suspended from
the saddle.

If the groom had seen the changes the girl made to her
appearance when in the area of woodland that surrounded and
offered privacy, he would have felt even greater disapproval

and probably no little concern over her electing to go there. First she took off and hung over a nearby bush the black masculine top hat with gray muslin fastened around the base and dangling almost to waist level down her back. These were placed with the headdress, but she retained her thin black leather gloves, as they were no impediment to freedom of movement by her hands. Using the blow to her head as an excuse, she had had her hair cut shorter than was currently considered fashionable although not to the extremes she would have it shorn later. The removal of the tight-waisted bodice and voluminous skirt of her modish and socially acceptable riding habit left her clad in an open-necked dark blue male shirt, snugly fitting black riding breeches, and the boots.

With the changes made to her appearance, Belle mounted the horse with none of the slight difficulty she had experienced as the result of wearing feminine attire in conjunction with a masculine type of saddle. Then, having paused for a moment she required to steel her resolve for what she was planning to do, she set the spirited bay moving. Rejoining the narrow track from which she had deviated so as to be able to leave her temporarily discarded garments in concealment from anybody who might pass before she returned, she soon came into sight of her destination. It was a mansion somewhat smaller than Baton Royale Manor or the Thatchers' home, but gave indications of being equally well maintained.

There was nothing about it to suggest that the purposes to which the building was put by its owner were far different from those of any of his neighbors. However, Belle was aware—as were all the local women of her class with whom she was acquainted—that it was run as an establishment devoted to gambling by its owner. She was equally cognizant of the fact that, having been discharged from the United States Army by a court-martial following an accusation of cheating in a poker game for high stakes and acquiring the reputation for being a successful duelist with two fatalities to his credit, the man she was visiting was regarded as persona non grata by well-raised feminine society throughout the whole of Baton Bayou Parish.

Bringing the roan gelding to a halt in front of the main entrance to the property, Belle was amused by the reaction

from the young Negro who came running up on discovering
that she was a young woman dressed in masculine attire and
having weapons fastened to her saddle. However, having said
that he thought she could have come to the wrong place, without explaining why he had reached such a conclusion, he offered to take charge of the animal. Remarking that she was
unsure of how long her business with Captain de-Farge would
take, she removed the sword and pistols from the rig and sur-
rendered the reins. Shaking his head in puzzlement instead of
making any further comment, the man proceeded to lead the
horse around the end of the building in a way that suggested
it was a regular part of his duties. Feeling sure her mount
would receive the best of attention, she walked across the
porch and, placing the weapons where they would not be seen
by whoever came in answer to her summons, used the large
well-polished brass knocker in the shaped of a stylized face of
the Devil.

"Abandon hope all ye who enter here," Belle mused with
a wry smile as she listened to the clatter she was making. "Oh
well, I've only myself to blame for coming."

"It's too early in the d—!" announced an irate feminine
voice with what the girl recognized as being an English accent
that had the suggestion of some culture and refinement acquired by practice rather than as a result of having been to the
manner born. Then there was the sound of the big door being
unlocked and bolts were withdrawn so the door could be
drawn open a short way. Clad in a pink negligee that left little
about her close-to-buxom and firmly fleshed physical attributes
to the imagination and very little else except for open-toed and
high-heeled white mules on her otherwise bare feet, a clearly
less-than-pleased woman looked out. Her hair, which was of
a hue suggestive in its redness of being in part achieved by
the use of henna, was rumpled and her face devoid of the
makeup it would almost certainly have in other circumstances.
Showing an increasing disdain, she ran her gaze up and down
in a way Belle found to be most annoying. "Oh, you're one
of *them*, are you?"

"I beg your pardon?" the girl queried, genuinely puzzled
by the cryptic way in which the statement was made.

"Sorry, girlie," the redhead said, still showing the superciliousness. "You've come to the wrong place. We only offer gambling and the occasional bout of fisticuffs for our gentlemen guests. Mrs. Jackson's the one you want to go and see to play *those* kind of games."

"Just a *moment*!" Belle snapped, knowing the woman who had been named ran what was politely termed a "house of ill repute" despite the pretense of being an actress. Belle was not sufficiently lacking in world matters that she failed to understand the implication of the explanation. "I want to see Captain de-Farge."

"I just *bet* you do, *girlie*," the redhead sneered, and she started to close the door.

Before the move could be completed, the door was given a push by the slender girl with such force that the woman involuntarily took a couple of paces backward to avoid being struck by it.

"I said I want to see Captain de-Farge," Belle stated grimly, taking grave exception to the way she was being addressed and stepping across the threshold into what she guessed must be the main entrance hall of the building. Annoyed by the greeting she had received and the thoughts that motivated it, she failed to notice that the furnishings and appointments were all in excellent taste even by the strictest conventional requirements. Nevertheless, she was not unaware that half a dozen shapely women clad in an equally revealing fashion and a bulky old Negro in the attire of a footman were watching from the open door of what appeared to be a dining room. "So will you *please*—!"

"All right, *girlie*!" the redhead interrupted, the same emphasis continuing to be placed upon the clearly insulting designation. Clenching her right hand into a fist and looking menacing, she went on, "No matter how big and high muckity-muck your momma and poppa might be hereabouts, you've asked for—!"

Despite knowing that the words were spoken without the redhead's being aware of who she was and how recently she had lost her parents, Belle responded to the implied threat. Realizing how dangerous the action she contemplated would prove to be if carried out against the woman, particularly as she believed it would be completely unexpected, she began to

move. Pivoting with a close-to-balletic grace similar to that
displayed to Auntie Mattie against the modified tailor's female
dummy in her sitting room, she sent her right foot crashing at
face height against the wooden panels of the main entrance.
There was a resounding crack as the sole and heel of the riding
boot made the contact and, its sturdy bulk notwithstanding, the
door jerked with some violence in response to the impact.

"All right, *girlie*!" Belle said, her voice and manner indicative of a still-controlled yet potentially dangerous anger,
as her foot returned to the floor. "I still mean to see Captain
de-Farge and *you* aren't capable of stopping me, nor even
dressed for trying."

Staring at the mark left by the boot on the panel that was
struck by the swiftly performed and clearly very powerful
kick, the redhead found herself on the horns of a dilemma.
While her every instinct warned that she had been told the
truth about her attire should she elect to take physical action
against the young and slender visitor, she had the reputation
for toughness she had acquired, and that—along with a close
relationship with her employer—gave her considerable moral
ascendancy over her fellow female workers in the gambling
house. If she refused to take up the challenge, she would suffer
a serious loss of faith with them. On the other hand, competent
though she knew herself to be at engaging in physical conflict
against other members of her sex under more normal conditions, she felt sure the kick had not been made by chance.
Rather, it was performed by one very well versed in such
matters and whose footwear would allow the knowledge to be
exploited to damaging and most painful purpose.

Aware that she was being watched with eager anticipation
by the women with whom she had been taking breakfast, the
redhead wondered how she might extricate herself from the
predicament of her own making without her standing among
them suffering an adverse effect.

CHAPTER SEVEN

Teach Me All *You* Know

"Well now, Roxanne my little spitfire, whatever are you up to *this* time?"

Never had the well-mannered Southern drawl with its slight suggestion of the French-Creole patois of her employer sounded so welcome to the redheaded woman who called herself Roxanne Fortescue-Smethers and declared her ancestral home to be Belvior—which she always said was pronounced "Beaver"—Castle in Nottingham, England, despite having been born Bertha Smith, but in a less exalted part of the same city where, however, the high-class residence she claimed was not situated.

Nor was Belle Boyd any less pleased to see the man from whom she had come to ask a favor.

The girl had not wished to jeopardize her chance by being compelled to defend herself against and possibly inflict serious injury upon one of his female employees.

Although Captain Anatol de-Farge generally dressed after the fashion of a wealthy Southern plantation owner, because the hour was early as he judged the time of the day, he was not wearing a jacket, collar, or tie and had on carpet slippers instead of his usual well-polished brown Hessian leg riding boots. He was tall, handsome in a somewhat swarthy Gallic fashion, with a slender build suggestive of wiry strength and agility, neither of which traits was lacking in his bodily makeup, as he always kept himself in the peak of physical condition. Regardless of his being a professional gambler and the owner of a well-known establishment offering a variety of games of chance along with other diversions for those wealthy enough to afford his high prices, he still bore himself with the carriage of the professional soldier he had been until a scandal and court-martial blasted his promising career.

"Good heavens!" the gambler almost gasped before the

redhead could reply, having turned his gaze in Belle's direction. "Is that really *you*, Miss Boyd?"

"I'm afraid it is," the girl replied, noticing that there was
a suggestion of disapproval in the way she was addressed.

"Miss *Boyd*?" Roxanne repeated, and a change to contri-
tion came into her voice as she continued, "I'm sorry for what
I said about your parents, Miss Boyd, but I didn't realize who
you are."

"That's all right," Belle asserted, not sorry for the hostility
shown by the redhead to be ended in a way that would cause
none of the loss of respect she had been trying to avoid. "You
weren't to know. I thought I would attract less attention looking the way I do if I should be seen coming here."

"May I ask *why* you have come, Miss Boyd?" de-Farge
requested, but did not wait for an answer before looking at the
scantily attired women in a pointed fashion and saying,
"Shouldn't you be finishing your breakfast, my angels, then
getting yourselves ready for the afternoon's activities?"

"Come on, girls," the redhead ordered, speaking as im-
periously as usual, while watching for any suggestions that her
authority over the other women had been reduced by the in-
decision she had shown when issued what amounted to an
open challenge in their circles from the slender girl. Seeing
none, even from her closest rival, she went on, "Let's go and
do it."

"Perhaps you would care to speak with me in my private
office, Miss Boyd?" the gambler suggested, watching the
girl's face with the keen eye of a man who made much of his
living by studying and seeking to assess human emotions. "I
can ask Roxanne, or one of the other ladies, as a chaperone if
you wish."

"There's no need for that, sir," Belle replied.

"One of my French bloodline might take exception to that
from an attractive young lady like yourself," de-Farge claimed
with a smile, contriving to sound even more Gallic than ever.
"Or one far less attractive than yourself even, provided her . . .
balance was of a satisfactory nature."

"I really wouldn't know what you mean, sir," the girl answered, finding herself liking the man who many women of

her class would have considered undesirable company for her. Allowing herself to be guided toward an inconspicuous door with nothing to indicate its purpose at one side of the entrance hall, she continued, "And I really must apologize for coming here the way I have."

"You certainly gave dear Roxanne the wrong impression," the gambler said, still smiling in a warm way that relieved some of the professional inscrutability from his handsome face and giving a hint of the kind of man he used to be during his early days in the Army. Opening the door and allowing Belle to precede him through it, he went on, "And, good as I know she is in such matters, I'm pleased she didn't take up your challenge. I have seldom seen the *chasse croise* of savate performed with such grace and power and nev—!"

"And never by a mere *woman*," the girl finished the incomplete sentence, but without any suggestion of having taken offense.

"I would never call you 'mere,' Miss Boyd," de-Farge claimed, having seated his guest. "May I have coffee or anything else brought in for you?"

"No, thank you," Belle refused politely. "I took breakfast with Colonel and Mrs. Thatcher before I left to visit you."

"I'm afraid that early to bed, early to rise has never been one of my many good points," the gambler declared, then he became sober. "Please forgive me for being so remiss. My condolences upon the death of your parents."

"Thank you, sir," Belle said formally, knowing the sentiment was sincere.

"Your father was far too wise to honor me by his presence at my tables," de-Farge stated without rancor. "But I respected him as a damned fine gentleman."

"Again, sir, my thanks," Belle said, and was sincere. "He felt the same way about you. In fact, he always used to tell our young guests—and some who were not so young—that if they had to gamble, to come and do it with you."

"He had such trust in me?"

"A friend of ours, Joe Brambile, with whom I am sure you are acquainted, always used to say that, like himself, you knew the percentages were so favorable in your behalf that you had no reason to cheat and, when he explained what he meant to me, I agreed there was none.''[1]

"I know Joe and I'm honored that I have your respect," the gambler declared. "Damn it, ma'am, if I'd only known what those two Yankee no-bullfighter bas—what they planned, I would have made sure they never had a chance to even think of looking for the help they got for doing it."

"They came *here*?" Belle asked, eager to know anything that might help her to trace Tollinger and Barmain. "No disrespect to your establishment, sir, but what little I saw and have learned about them wouldn't have led me to think they were the kind to come gambling in such a highly priced place."

"They certainly wouldn't have gone to dear Glenda's for their pleasure," de-Farge claimed dryly. "Regardless of what Roxanne told you regarding the way you're dressed, she doesn't cater for anything except straight man and wom—!"

"I know who she is and what you mean," Belle asserted with a smile. "Momma and Auntie Mattie thought I should know even the more seamy facts of life. Anyway, you say Tollinger and Barmain have been here."

"Only a couple of times," de-Farge confirmed. "And not to preach the kind of 'liberal' garbage they were giving out along the river, going by all I heard. Each time, what they lost hardly covered the broke money they asked for and the meals they had on the house. That kind of business—and customers—I can do without. Anyway, how may I be of service to you?"

"Do you have any idea where they could have gone after they ran away from our home?" Belle wanted to know.

"I'm afraid not, except that I would say it would have to be back up north," the gambler answered. "Only, I don't think you came here to ask about them, interested as I know you must be in trying to have them located."

---

[1] *Information about some incidents in the career of professional gambler Joseph "Joe" Brambile is given in* DOC LEROY, M.D.; THE HIDE AND HORN SALOON; *and* Part Two, "Jordan's Try," THE TOWN TAMERS.

"It isn't," Belle admitted. "I would like you to teach me fencing."

"Going by all I've heard, Miss Boyd," de-Farge remarked, his face returning to being an imperturbable mask, "your father taught you how to use a sword and you've got to be pretty good at it."

"Poppa taught me all he knew," Belle admitted. "But I would like you to teach me all *you* know. With what I have to do, should I need to use a sword, it won't be for formal dueling, and I've already learned just how much difference there is between fencing practice and using a sword for what it is really meant. What I can learn from you could make the difference between life and death for me."

"So you want to know how to fight by foul methods," de-Farge declared rather than asked, his face remaining an expressionless mask. "And your father didn't know enough about them to teach you, but you feel sure I *can*."

"I'm not so foolishly naive that I believe all those hotheads who live for the *code duello* are noble sportsmen who stick to the rules at all times," Belle pointed out, realizing how the reason for her request could be interpreted and seeking to make amends for any offense she may have inadvertently caused. "And I'm aware that a man who has gained a reputation as a duelist is sometimes challenged by men seeking to gain a reputation by defeating him to such an extent that they don't care what means they use to bring it about. It's the same as Joe Brambile says about cheating at gambling: he doesn't do it—or you either—but you have to know how it can be done to stop others doing it to you."

"Joe has a good point, I'll admit."

"I've always felt so, and Poppa always used to tell me that if you want to learn something, go to somebody who knows what it is all about. Well, I may need to know how to fight any way I have to if I want to stay alive and do what I mean to do."

"You're going after Tollinger and Barmain?" the gambler said, once again making the words more statement than question.

"I've no brothers to do it," the girl replied quietly. "And, as I told Reverend Jacob, Poppa always raised me for the son he never had, so it's up to me to avenge his and Momma's murder.''

"Then I'll do as you wish," de-Farge promised, and a faint smile came to his lips. "May I ask if you will do something for me in return?"

"Of course I will."

"You may not approve when you hear what it is."

"You probably don't *really* approve of teaching me how to fight by foul means—and not because you object to giving away what might be called trade secrets," Belle countered. "So what can I do for you?"

"I have a slender young Irish girl who looks like butter wouldn't melt in her mouth and even Roxanne is rather careful not to antagonize," the gambler explained. "She likes nothing more than to fight with other women, and I have a rival with a lady for whom he has the greatest regards along the same lines. If Andrea had at least some of your skill at savate—!"

"It would give her what I've heard you gambling men call a decided edge," the girl guessed. "So you want me to teach her savate and will make money by betting on her to win a fight?"

"I have something like that in mind," de-Farge admitted with a grin.

"There are some who would say doing it would smack of sharp practice," Belle pointed out, but she too was smiling. "Would you stoop to such a thing?"

"I *never* stoop, ma'am," de-Farge asserted. "It's just that, as you suspect, I prefer a reasonable edge, as I have never believed in gambling if doing so was avoidable at any point of my life. That is why I run this house instead of playing in one owned by somebody else."

*   *   *

"And now, gentlemen, for the main attraction of the evening. The settling of an affair of honor between Lady Roxanne Fortescue-Smethers and her unknown assailant, whose identity will only be exposed to you if she loses, Madame Mask!"

Standing with her shoulders resting against the soft cloth sack filled with cotton hanging over the wooden post in one corner of the raised dais at the center of the main room of Captain Anatol de-Farge's gambling house, Belle Boyd had never before appeared in public wearing such scanty and revealing attire. With her hair—which had been dyed blond— drawn back and held by a strip of black cloth in the way a later generation would call a ponytail, her face was covered, except for her eyes, nostrils, and mouth, by a silk mask of the same material. She was clad in a figure-hugging sleeveless and white cotton bodice with a more extreme décolleté than anything she had previously even seen, short-legged matching pantalets, and ballet slippers without padded points on her otherwise bare feet. Conscious of the lascivious scrutiny to which she was being subjected by the male occupants, she thought wryly that she had only herself to blame for being there clad in such a fashion.

Accepting the offer of assistance for Andrea that the girl had given, the gambler had commenced her first lesson in fighting rather than merely fencing. By the time she left for the Thatcher mansion in the evening, she had already started to acquire some of the basics of less-than-sporting combat with an *épée de combat*. She had also found her pupil for lessons in savate to be equally enthusiastic over the possibility of using such methods in physical conflict against other female opponents and eager to learn all she could teach. The eagerness displayed by the slender and agile brown-haired Irish youngster toward the thought of fighting members of their sex had done much to remove the misgivings she had had when agreeing to supply the instruction. Therefore, de-Farge had found he had two willing pupils seeking to acquire knowledge— albeit in different subjects and for diverse purposes—working with assiduity under his roof.

With the exception of Sundays, for the past four weeks Belle had spent from nine in the morning until five in the evening at the gambling house. Having been summoned on the first Sunday to meet Mattie Jonias at the house on the Baton Royale estate where she was recovering from the gunshot wound, the girl had discovered that she knew what was taking place. What was more important where Belle was concerned had been that the elderly Negress not only guessed why she was behaving in such a fashion, but—despite the disapproval often shown over her less-than-ladylike activities before the attack on her home—stated unqualified agreement with what she hoped to achieve. There had been an added benefit for the girl in addition to receiving the approbation from Auntie Mattie. Word had been spread among the other colored folks by her former ''mammy'' that whatever Miss Belle did was to be treated as a secret not to be disclosed under any circumstances. Therefore, she knew that she need not fear even accidental exposure by any of them and also was given cooperation by all the grooms at her temporary residence when she went to collect her horse each day.

Not only had de-Farge been as good as his word when agreeing to teach Belle the secrets of the professional duelist who sought to gain an unfair advantage when engaged in what was supposed to be an affair of honor—in the acquiring of all of which she had proved herself a most adept pupil whether with sword, pistol, or fighting knife—of his own free will and making no suggestion of requiring payment, but he provided several items that he claimed might be of use in her quest. That he had them in his possession implied he had at some time had the acquaintance of a woman who had a decided instinct for self-preservation coupled with an absence of moral scruples.

There was a bracelet of copper treated to give the appearance of looking gold that had a section of the upper edge rendered razor-sharp, allowing it to be used as an effective slashing weapon when she had gained the knack of wielding it. Possibly having been made with the intention of seeing identifying marks on the backs of a deck of cards, the pendant of a costly gold locket had a glass front that could be opened to serve as a powerful magnifying glass. What appeared to be an ordinary ring had a large apparently diamond stone that, when moved aside, allowed enough of a powdered opiate—a supply of which the gambler provided—from a space below it to render a human being unconscious when dropped into a drink.

Saying the effects produced upon unsuspecting members of his sex were sure to make doing so worthwhile, the gambler had also made a suggestion that Belle adopted and was to put to good use on numerous occasions for the remainder of her life. This was to have the waistband of her skirts modified so they could be liberated and would fall to allow her legs greater freedom of movement than was possible while the garment was in its usual place. He also suggested she should have underneath either the snugly fitting riding breeches and calf-high boots or—which he claimed he considered as creating an even more salutary result—the most daring nether garments she could obtain, along with black stockings supported by brightly colored suspender straps.

Such was the eagerness with which Belle absorbed all her lessons, by the end of the fourth week de-Farge had stated that he could teach her nothing further. What was more, the instructions at employing savate and a few other bare-handed fighting tricks that were supplied to Andrea had reached the point where he considered her to be ready to carry out the purpose for which she was being trained. Therefore, accepting the assessment, he had arranged for the bout to take place on a Saturday evening when he knew it would attract a large number of spectators who would become players at the various games of chance he offered.

Wanting to see the results of her efforts where Andrea was concerned, for the first time in her association with the owner Belle had remained at the gambling house in the evening. Then a snag had arisen. Claiming that his contender had sustained an accident while in training, the man upon whom de-Farge was hoping to gain an advantage in betting sent word that the bout would have to be delayed. Knowing of the interest aroused by word having been passed that such an event would be forthcoming, but wanting to keep the capabilities of the Irish girl undiscovered, the gambler had decided to employ substitutes.

Learning that the redhead was to be one contender and remembering the way in which they had first met, despite having learned how skimpily whoever was involved would be attired, it had been with a sense of impish perversity that Belle offered to be the other participant. When de-Farge warned that there were sure to be men with whom she was acquainted among the spectators, she had suggested a means by which she could avoid being recognized. She had realized that the stipulation of the mask being removed in the event of her losing could circumvent the scheme to keep her identity a secret, but had stated that this gave her an added incentive to become the winner.

The time had come for the commencement of the bout, and Belle was unable to prevent a slight apprehension as she considered the outcome should she lose.

CHAPTER EIGHT

Let's Give Them a *Show*

Thrusting herself forward on the order to commence the bout being given by the small man who had been introduced as "Our Referee, Mr. Horatio Hislop," Belle Boyd put the plan of campaign she had formulated into effect. She had already tested and found to her liking the surface of what she had been informed by Captain Anatol de-Farge was called a ring and what came into regular use elsewhere for carrying out bare-fisted pugilism or wrestling between men. Beneath the smooth cloth stretched tightly across all of it was a three-inch-deep layer of straw spread to an even thickness. This was only one of the precautions that had been taken to reduce the chance of either combatant being injured in the fighting.

Although she had had no experience in such matters, even at second hand through hearing anything of the kind discussed around the fire on a hunting expedition—where various unusual types of sport or entertainment were occasionally the subject of conversation—Belle could not find fault with the way in which the bout was to be conducted. In addition to both having their fingernails cut down and filed smooth, they were wearing white cotton gloves to further prevent scratches from being delivered in a way that could leave disfiguring scars. They had also been informed by the referee of the kind of tactics, including biting and eye-gouging, that were not permissible. For the rest, they were instructed to continue their struggles until one was unable to continue or stated she wished to surrender.

Darting toward Roxanne Fortescue-Smethers, who was dressed in the same way as herself except for her garments being bright blue, Belle watched the way she was being approached. The good-looking and curvaceously close-to-buxom redhead clearly had had considerable experience in such affairs and was moving in a slightly crouching posture with hands

held slightly ahead, ready to take whatever action she felt the
situation required. What Roxanne did not anticipate was the
way the slender and, as she had had her eighteenth birthday
shortly after the murder of her parents, twelve-years-younger
girl was intending.

Just before the outstretched hands could reach her, Belle
sprang into the air, putting to use the agility she had acquired
in the course of her active life. Acting as if engaged in a game
of leapfrog, placing her hands on top of the unsecured mass
of red hair as an aid to what she was doing, she passed over
her amazed opponent's head. On descending, to the accom-
paniment of surprised yet delighted utterances from the spectators that turned to laughter, she pivoted and delivered a kick
to Roxanne's thinly covered, plumply well-rounded rump.
Driven onward with little control over her movements, such
was the surprise she had received, the redhead was brought to
a halt by the post in the corner her opponent had left so speed-
ily. Spluttering a profanity that was justifiable under the circumstances, she turned around in a defensive posture as she
was expecting to be attacked.

Finding that the girl was standing with feet spread apart
and arms akimbo in the center of the ring, contriving to exude
an annoying suggestion of satisfaction in spite of the mask
concealing her facial expression, Roxanne rushed forward.
Once again, her attempt to come into contact failed. Moving
aside before a hand could be laid upon her, Belle snapped a
horizontal side kick that took the passing redhead in the pit of
the stomach. Because the speed of the movement robbed the
attack of much of its potency, its recipient gave a gasp more
of frustration and anger than pain. Although not seriously hurt,
the redhead was unable to prevent herself from starting to fold
at the waist. On doing so, having inadvertently offered the
target, she received another kick to the rump and was sent
back to the corner she had been assigned. Once again, the
padded sack saved her from going farther. Spluttering more
angry exclamations, she twisted around and discovered that
the girl had once again halted instead of following her to make
the most of the advantage that had been gained.

Instinctively starting to move forward with the same speed
as before, the redhead watched Belle adopt what—although

she did not know it—was the left fighting stance of savate. Body erect, with most of her weight equally distributed on the balls of her feet, she had the left toes pointing forward, the center of the right at about shoulder width apart, and the knees slightly bent. This caused her to be standing slightly sideways so as to offer less of her torso as a target for hostile action. Her head was up, eyes directed at her opponent's chest. With her elbows pointing down, she kept them close to her sides, and her forearms—the hands clenched into fists—were vertical to the ground so the left was just below eye level and the right gave cover for her solar plexus.

Despite never having come into contact with such a posture and knowing nothing of the lessons that had been given to the Irish girl, de-Farge wanting to avoid any chance of even an unintended disclosure of the way Andrea was being trained, Roxanne accepted that she was up against a very competent opponent in the slender and beautiful Southron. The supposition was given support by Belle, who, instead of waiting for the redhead to come to her, darted forward and sent her left foot in a *chasse croise* kick similar to the one used with the front entrance of the house as a target on the day of her first visit. Fortunately for Roxanne, once more the speed of delivery reduced the force and the bottom of her chin was caught with much less force than caused the door to respond so violently. In spite of this, she found herself being propelled backward until once again she was brought into contact—her shoulders making it this time—with the padded cover of the corner post.

On the point of advancing to deliver what she believed would prove to be a coup de grâce, the redhead clearly having no conception of how to cope with attacks by savate, Belle realized what achieving victory in such an easy fashion would do. From what de-Farge had said, Roxanne was a regular competitor in such bouts and had never been beaten. He also claimed that this allowed her to keep the other women under a control that was beneficial to the smooth running of his establishment and that she received extra pay for doing so. Belle suddenly became aware that suffering defeat in such an easy fashion would result in her losing authority over the other female members of the staff, and she had no wish for this to happen.

Apart from the first incivility, for which Belle had received an apology and agreed with the motivation after learning what had caused the reception—as she, too, had a healthy distaste for the kind of sexual deviation she was thought to be seeking—Roxanne had treated her with courtesy on all their encounters, while not behaving in a subservient fashion. Certainly nothing had happened to make the girl feel her opponent deserved to be treated in a fashion that would cause her humiliation and the loss of the position in the establishment that she held in a most satisfactory fashion, according to the gambler. The only problem facing Belle was whether she could allow the redhead such an opportunity to fight back without becoming the loser and being compelled by the rules to have her mask removed, since there were at least half a dozen of the men crowding the room who would recognize her.

Never one to worry about what might happen, the girl darted forward and grabbed Roxanne by the hair. Although slightly affected by the *chasse croise* kick, the redhead was not too dazed to appreciate the chance she was being offered. In fact, she was relieved that something much more effective and painful was not being inflicted by the obviously capable young Southron over whom she had expected to obtain an easy victory. Just as she was about to respond in kind, she received a surprise.

"Are you able to go on struggling, Roxanne? If not, what can I do to help you?"

Suddenly realizing what was implied by the the words, which were pitched so low that not even Hislop—who she knew would keep well clear unless the far-from-comprehensive rules were being infringed—could hear, the redhead understood what was implied by them. It was obvious to her that the girl was wanting to know whether she was capable of continuing the bout, and she instinctively guessed that this was not due to wanting to continue the humiliating treatment. Sending her fingers into Belle's black locks, she gave an equally *sotto voce* answer in the affirmative.

"Good!" Belle breathed, still just loud enough for her opponent to hear. "Let's give them a *show*!"

Contriving to look as if the pulling they were doing was far more painful than was the case, the combatants went in a twirlin rush toward the center of the ring. Then, entangling their legs, they fell to the padded surface of the ring to commence a wild yet harmless struggling mill that took them over and over in what appeared to be the primitively instinctive manner of women without training when engaged in physical conflict. Among the screeches and squeals that both were emitting, without letting the words be heard by anybody other than Belle, the redhead contrived to thank her for her consideration and began to give suggestions of how they should continue the action for the benefit of the audience.

Considering that the girl had never indulged in anything of the kind, although the redhead admitted later that the majority of her bouts against the other female members of the establishment were carried out in such a fashion, they contrived to put on what appeared to be a vigorously conducted struggle that the audience clearly never suspected was other than genuine.[1] Nevertheless, there was one aspect of the supposed conflict that Belle found disconcerting, since she had not been warned by de-Farge that it might happen. In the course of the mill on the floor, without letting it be seen she was doing so, Roxanne had contrived to rip open the front of her flimsy bodice so her big and firmly jutting bosom was brought into view.

When asked in the same surreptitious fashion whether she wanted to call off the struggling until the damage could be corrected, she replied that having it occur was an accepted part of the action and that its subsequent removal was all the loss of attire that would take place. Realizing that the perspiration she was already shedding freely must have rendered her own garments as sodden as and even more revealing than the redhead's attire, and having no feelings of false modesty in consideration of the way she was already behaving, Belle said she was willing to be stripped to the waist if this too would be accepted, and this was done in a suitably realistic and supposedly unexpected fashion.

Although Belle would be forced into physical conflict

---

[1] *How the participants in the so-called "apartment-house wrestling" by a later generation carried out a similar judicious faking is told in* THE TEAM, *the latest volume to be added to the* Rockabye County *series.*

against other women more than once, there would be only two
occasions in the future when she was compelled by circumstances to indulge in such less-than-serious conflict.[2] However,
despite this being the first time she had done anything of the
kind and there having been no suggestion of it happening before the bout commenced, given support by the much more
experienced redhead—who was not averse to carrying out the
usual kind of simulated fighting after the effective way in
which the opening moves were made against her—the girl was
able to put on a most convincing performance. Putting to use
the latent histrionic ability that would serve her so well in her
future career, Belle was able to simulate all the emotions that
were required, whether suggesting delight at success, frustration when some move she was making was thwarted, or the
appropriate response when she was subjected to some form of
gently applied suffering. The latter was shown to good advantage when, having whispered that such was expected by the
spectators, Roxanne grabbed and appeared to be subjecting her
bare breasts to a grinding and twisting that looked much more
painful than was the case. The kick she sent between the redhead's thighs to bring about the release from the hold appeared
equally hurtful without being so.

Continuing to be guided by Roxanne without any of the
spectators realizing this was taking place, Belle put all her best
efforts into helping produce a clearly well-enjoyed simulation
of fighting. Having learned that such was always considered
amusing by the audience, the redhead was pretending to remove the girl's mask without having attained the requisite victory. On the referee trying to stop this happening, they turned
upon him and, taking him to the floor with them, appeared to
be subjecting him to a mauling instead of each other.

Leaving Hislop behind after a few seconds, which was
greeted by amused comments from the onlookers, the combatants rolled away in their still well-simulated basic feminine
conflict. Doing so inadvertently took them under the lowest
rope, so they carried on their supposed fighting outside the

[2] *The occasions when Belle Boyd was required to indulge in less-than-
serious bare-handed combat with another woman are described in* THE
BAD BUNCH *and* THE WHIP AND THE WAR LANCE.

ring. This lasted for a few seconds before the nearest spectators, one of whom was an acquaintance of Belle but gave not
the slightest suggestion of recognizing her—which was not
surprising due to the mask, the change made to the color of
her hair as an aid to avoiding her identity being disclosed, and
her skimpily dressed condition—as she screeched out protests
in a more coarse-sounding voice than was her usual tone, combined to separate and return them to the ring. Once there, with
Hislop keeping well clear once more, they resumed their efforts with vim and vigor.

Watching what was taking place in the ring, de-Farge
quickly began to lose the concern and even twinges of conscience he had experienced over having allowed himself to be
persuaded by Belle to let her be a participant in the bout.
Despite having seen how capably she could perform savate,
he had wondered whether she could put her knowledge to
serious use against another woman. What was more, he was
aware of how competent Roxanne was in such events and had
no wish to see the Southron girl—for whom he had developed
a great admiration during their comparatively short acquaintance—sustain injury because of inexperience. Once the action
commenced, he had soon concluded that he had nothing to
fear on either account. However, he had grown less certain
when Belle began to indulge in the kind of struggling that he
believed would be more in the favor of the redhead.

So skillfully had the faking of the fighting been done, it
had taken the gambler several seconds to become aware that
the combatants were not engaged in serious and determined
conflict. However, as it was continued with vigor and what
appeared to be authenticity—apart from having qualms when
Belle joined the redhead in being bared to the waist until he
realized that, like everything else now happening between
them, it had been done deliberately at her instigation—he
found himself growing increasingly satisfied by what was taking place. Not one of the spectators was giving the slightest
indication of suspecting other than genuine action. Furthermore, obviously by mutual consent, the pair took turns in becoming dominant in the action to the point where defeat for
one seemed imminent until being averted by the other apparently turning the tables and briefly gaining the upper hand.

Such supposed fluctuations on behalf of the combatants were beneficial to the wagering that was taking place, enough bets being placed with de-Farge or his employees for him to be able to foresee a profitable evening. However, as he was thinking with some satisfaction on those lines, he realized that there was one snag that neither he nor, he suspected, the pair in the ring had taken into account. The reason for having had Belle's hair dyed blond and her face concealed by the mask, which the redhead on two occasions appeared to be trying to remove until prevented by Hislop in accordance with the instructions he had been given, was to prevent her from being recognized. However, under the terms announced for the bout, the covering would be taken off in the event of her losing.

Having no desire to have the girl's identity exposed, the gambler wondered how this might be averted without arousing objections from the audience.

The same problem had occurred to Belle and Roxanne.

What was more, the girl and the redhead had arrived at what they considered to be the best possible solution.

After some eight minutes of action, during which the pair had successfully avoided letting it become obvious that neither was trying to hurt the other despite each giving the impression she was determined to achieve victory, they were showing the effects of their strenuous activities. This went beyond each's hair being reduced to a sodden tangle and bodies soaked by copiously shed perspiration, which had a detrimental effect upon their far-from-extensive solitary surviving item of attire, now reduced to a state of near immodesty beyond anything Belle imagined. They were growing so exhausted that each realized she might inadvertently give or sustain the kind of injury they wanted to avoid being inflicted. With that in mind, after a brief and still-unobserved discussion, they set about putting the scheme they had produced into effect.

Coming to their feet on genuinely wobbling legs due to their now-enfeebled state after another session of rolling around on the floor of the ring, the disheveled and close-to-exhausted pair staggered apart. However, their separation was brief. Moving in, each swung a punch in a manner redolent of their physically drained condition. Nevertheless, like the blows and kicks they had essayed earlier, with Belle contriving to pull her own as effectively and comparatively harmlessly as Roxanne was doing despite having had no training in such matters, the punch that each launched was delivered in an authentic-seeming fashion.

The fact that the pair swung with much less than their earlier vigor was accepted by the spectators as being excusable under the circumstances. Arriving almost simultaneously in closer to a push than a blow, the simulated attacks allowed the recipients to go down on their backs and lie with limbs spread-eagled, as if they had been rendered unconscious. Having examined them, Hislop declared that neither would be able to resume the fighting and, therefore, the bout was a draw. Calling for applause for two very gallant ladies, de-Farge stated that in view of the indecisive result, Madame Mask would not have her features exposed. Before any objections could be raised, he asked whether a second bout would be welcomed and the affirmative response ensured that Belle's participation would never be discovered.

It was, although neither the girl nor the gambler realized the point, an example of the lengths to which she would be willing to go to achieve her ends when she became the Rebel Spy.

CHAPTER NINE

You Could Be What I Want

"I'm really sorry, Belle," Colonel Myles Raines declared, looking as impassively as he could manage at the slender and straight-backed beautiful girl who was standing on the other side of his desk. He had known her family for years and was aware that she was not more than three years older than his daughter, Louise.[1] For all that, she had an air of quietly grim determination beyond her years, and he could sympathize with her reasons for coming to see him even though he was unable to give her the assistance she required. "But there really is nothing I can do to help you."

"But there must be *some* way I can serve," Belle Boyd insisted, having told her reason for coming to Richmond, Virginia, without holding back the fact that she wanted to find and take revenge upon the men who had killed her parents.

With the completion of one specialized side of her education and having repaid her debt to Captain Anatol de-Farge for it by providing him with a very well received piece of entertainment, the girl had felt she was at last ready to commence her quest after Alfred Tollinger and George Barmain. Despite having been spurred on by Mattie Jonias, whose authority had not diminished while she was recovering from the wound received on the night of the attack upon Baton Royale Manor, the Negroes who worked the riverboats and did the necessary traveling were unable to find out more than that the pair had gone northward for some undiscovered destination. Therefore, especially with the commencement of hostilities between what amounted to the Southern and Northern states, she had accepted that she must take up the pursuit herself.

[1] *Information about the later careers of Colonel Myles Raines and his daughter, Louise, can be found in* WAGONS TO BACKSIGHT *and* RETURN TO BACKSIGHT; *also by inference with regard to the Colonel in* ARIZONA RANGE WAR.

Satisfied that she could leave her family's plantation and workforce in the capable hands of Colonel Dennis Thatcher and his wife Margaret, Belle had gathered what she would want for the expedition—including the garments modified as was suggested by de-Farge and the items for self-protection he had supplied—and had set out upon her mission of vengeance. Accepting that to attempt anything in Baton Bayou Parish or the surrounding area would achieve nothing, she had headed for the place she concluded would offer her the kind of contacts to serve her needs. Her first attempts to see the kind of senior officers her instincts suggested were most suited for her purpose came to nothing. In each case, a subordinate had informed her politely but firmly that the man she wished to see was too fully occupied in the business of vitally important matters pertaining to conducting the hostilities against the Yankees. Being made aware of how difficult gaining access to the people she required was almost certain to be, she had contrived to gain admittance to Raines as an old friend of her family.

However, the interview was not going the way the girl had hoped might prove to be the case.

"Well," Raines said in tones redolent of doubt. Bareheaded and with his dark hair tinged at the temples by a touch of white, he was a tall, lean man in the cadet-gray dress uniform of the Confederate States Cavalry and bore the insignia of his rank on the stand-up collar and sleeves of his jacket. "There is always working as a nurse. However, despite all that was said about Florence Nightingale with the British wounded soldiers and sailors in the Crimean War, *that* is not highly regarded by many people as a suitable occupation for a Southern lady like yourself."

"I don't have being a *nurse* in mind," the girl stated, aware that such an occupation was still regarded by many men as being restricted to lower-class women, even though she did not subscribe to the point of view. "Necessary as I know it is and noble though I believe it to be, becoming one won't do anything to help me catch Tollinger and Barmain."

"From what you say, they fled north before the War started," Raines reminded. "Don't you think that puts them well beyond your reach?"

"I've heard we have some of our people working secretly in the North," Belle pointed out. "Is that true?"

"One hears such things said," the Colonel admitted in a noncommittal tone.

"Then they must be controlled by *somebody*, or at least send their information to somebody," the girl asserted. "And the most likely place to find that somebody is here in Richmond, as it is the Capital of the Confederate States and all our leading civil and military authorities are assembled here."

"I suppose this would be the most logical place to look, assuming such people do actually exist, and I'm not saying they do."

"Poppa often used to tell me about how most countries have what is known as a secret service to do work of that kind."

"One *hears* of such things," the Colonel conceded cautiously, sensing he could be getting on dangerous ground as there were already strong rumors that both the South and the North were operating such organizations.

"And I can't see our leaders failing to have one," Belle declared. "Do *you* know who the one in charge of our secret service might be, sir?"

"My dear young lady," Raines said, once more needing to control the smile he could feel welling inside him. "I'm just one colonel of many waiting to receive command of a regiment. I've *never* become involved in such things and hope I never have to be. It's a very dirty business by all accounts. Anyway, I would say the main purpose of a secret service is ensuring that it remains a secret."

"But surely you can give me just a hint where to start looking?"

"Not so much as the start of a hint, I'm afraid. If I were you, Belle, I would put the whole idea from my mind and find some other way of serving the South."

"And forget what Tollinger and Barmain did to Momma and Poppa?"

"I know you can never forget that," Raines stated gently. "But it would be a waste of a useful young life for you to spend it trying for something you'll never manage to achieve. I think you would be far better advised to go home and set

about rebuilding Baton Royale Mansion and keep cotton flowing to help our cause.''

"I suppose that is the only thing for me to do," Belle
replied with a sigh. "Well, I thank you for your time and
advice, sir. May I wish you every success with the regiment
you receive.''

"Only, my advice is what you most definitely are *not* going
to take," Raines said silently to himself as he watched the girl
walk from his office. "There's too much of Electra and Vincent Boyd in you for that. In fact, I'd be willing to bet that if
anybody could run down Tollinger and Barmain, you'd be the
one to do so. It's a pity in some ways that you won't ever be
given the chance.''

* * *

"Stand still and keep your hands well clear of your sides!"
Belle Boyd ordered, having turned up the flame of the night-
light on the bedside table with her left hand. "If you make a
hostile move, or try to escape, I'll shoot you in the stomach,
and don't think for a moment I couldn't do it.''

As the girl was increasing the illumination to investigate
the slight noises that had disturbed her thoughts while lying in
bed trying to get to sleep after another abortive evening's activities, her right thumb deftly cocked the Colt Model of 1851
revolver she had bought to replace the lighter-caliber weapon
brought from her bedroom by Mattie Jonias on the night her
parents were murdered. An instant later, so excellently attuned
was her coordination that she was pointing its three-inch-long
octagonal barrel—the original length of seven and a half
inches having been cut down, in accordance with her instructions, by the gunsmith from whom she purchased it, thereby
obviating the need to return it to the company's factory for the
modification she required in the interests of permitting greater
ease of concealment—steadily at the masculine figure who
had woken her while forcing open the window and climbing
through into the second-floor room she was occupying at the
Sandford Hotel.

Four weeks had elapsed since the girl had had her meeting
with Colonel Myles Raines. While it had proved to be unpro-
ductive otherwise, it had taught her one thing. She had realized

that if she could not obtain assistance from a man who had
been a good friend of her parents, she was unlikely to achieve
more positive results with strangers or even such casual acquaintances who were in positions of much greater authority
even than a colonel awaiting command of a Cavalry regiment.
She had quickly learned the truth of her assumption. Although
she had managed to obtain interviews with a few highly placed
members of the military and civilian politicians, the results
were invariably the same. From some, she was received with
politeness and had been allowed to say something of what she
hoped to receive, then was turned away with much the same
arguments used by Raines. Others merely stated that such matters were not for a beautiful young woman to attempt and
dismissed her with a suggestion of having matters of great
importance demanding their attention.

Although dissatisfied with the outcome of her efforts to
obtain some form of official assistance and sanction, the girl
was enough of a realist to understand the attitude behind the
refusals. In every case, the man with whom she spoke had
been raised in the tradition that a Southern woman—especially
a young one from her stratum of society—should confine her
activities to the home and considered what she wanted to do
was beyond the pale, regardless of how good her motives.
Deciding she must do something positive on her own account,
she had set about trying to achieve her purpose in a way she
hoped would bring her to the favorable attention of the members of the Confederate States Secret Service she felt certain
were engaged in seeking to counter their Yankee opposite
numbers in Richmond.

Having had a good education in formal as well as unconventional subjects, under the firm control of her mother, Belle
had always been allowed to make the most use of her initiative
instead of constantly seeking guidance from her elders. She
had put all these traits to use in seeking to attain her ends.
Having anticipated that the need might arise, she had brought
the attire appropriate to the various functions to which her
standing in the social circles of Baton Bayou Parish made her
welcome. At each, she had sought out such officers as she had
thought might lead her where she wanted to go and flirted with
each in the hope of gaining the information.

In addition, when not engaged in such a fashion, she had put to use her ability at acting and a basic skill in disguise to seeking sources at a lower level of the city's population. Dressed in a suitable fashion in garments she had purchased in stores catering to women with less affluent means than her own, she presented herself in a fitting manner for the different types of company she was joining. She had been helped by having frequently achieved acclaim for the way in which she played the part of serving girls in amateur dramatics and remembering the attitudes and modes of speech used by the women at the gambling house run by Anatol de-Farge.

Such was the skill Belle had displayed that she was confident she had aroused no suspicions as she went around the places where noncommissioned officers and enlisted men found diversions, she hoped to meet someone who could lead her in the direction she wanted. However, as was the case with her efforts at a higher stratum of society, she had been compelled to admit to herself that she was not meeting with any greater success where achieving her purpose was concerned. On the other hand, she had not concluded that her efforts were entirely wasted. The lessons she learned while carrying out the pose of being a girl from a working-class background could prove to be of use if she should attract the attention of and be accepted as a member of the Secret Service.

That evening the girl had returned to the Sandford Hotel earlier than she anticipated, due to the need to avoid possible arrest by the authorities following her having been compelled to use her skill at savate to dissuade the hostile intentions of a woman in a tavern who took exception to her presence and interest in a sergeant in the Artillery. Deciding against trying at a more exalted level that night, although she had been invited to attend a soiree where some officers she had not yet met would be among the guests and might provide what she wanted, she elected to go to bed and catch up on some sleep. The latter had not come when she heard the sounds that led her to make ready for the intruder.

* * *

"Take hit easy, missis!" a startled voice with an accent strange to Belle Boyd's ears requested hastily. "I hain't going to move, nor get 'ostile neither."

Standing by the window he had contrived to reach and open despite the room's being on the second floor of the building, the speaker was neither impressive nor menacing in appearance. Not more than five feet six at most, clad in a tightly fitting black woollen turtleneck sweater and matching trousers, and with light rubber-soled boots such as were often worn by savate boxers on his feet, he was slender and wiry in build. Although his manner of speech did not strike the girl as being of any Gallic variety with which she had come into contact, he had a French-style black beret on his head. Although covered by the kind of black cork white performers in minstrel shows often used, his sharp features reminded her of a weasel due to the alert way in which he was darting glances about him. She did not believe he would prove dangerous unless she gave him cause to become that way.

"Come over here," Belle commanded, contriving to slip from the bed without for a moment allowing the Colt to turn from its alignment.

"Whatever you say," the man answered, pronouncing the last word as "sie" and starting to obey. "I'm catched dead to rights. But Hi've got a wife 'n' seven little children and no way to kept 'em fe——!"

"What's wrong?" Belle asked as the words came to an abrupt end and the man, whose gaze had been running over her willowy curvaceous figure in the white diaphanous nightgown, which was all she had on, and who displayed a frank interest not in accord with his declaration regarding the possession of a wife and family, stared fixedly by her.

"His that your mum 'n' dad, missi—*miss*?" the intruder asked, continuing to add an *H* as he had done before, while also leaving off other letters, and pointed in a dramatic fashion to the framed tintype portrait of the girl's parents that was standing on the bedside table.

"It is," Belle confirmed, but she did not relax her vigilance. She guessed what was implied by the question and thought it could be a ruse to divert her attention long enough for some kind of action to be taken.

"Then might Hi be struck dahn dead on the bleeding spot!" the man declared with vehemence. "Hand I deserve it for trying to rob Vincent Boyd's daughter."

"You knew Pop—my father?"

"We only hever met the once, miss, but Hi'll *never* forget what 'e done for me."

"And what was that?"

"'E catched me out doing a climb after the family jewels what des Boys Gilbert was allus a-boastin' abart," the man explained. "Hi's had it propped up for me good 'n' proper by somebody's'd never steered me wrong in the past 'n' Hi was counting on making the big tickle. Which's what hus in my line of work calls what you've maybe 'eard of's a real valuable amarnt of loot."

"So *you* are the one!" Belle asserted, remembering having heard her father speak of the incident after she had worked out who had been meant by the way in which the intruder pronounced the name of Roger de Bois Gilbert.

"Hi says to meself, Hi says, 'Halfred 'Iggins, you've been 'n' gone 'n' copped your lot good 'n' proper this time' when your dad come in on me like what he done. 'You should never 'ave left good old London tahn.' "

"Did you tell him about your wife and seven children?" Belle inquired with a smile, and allowed the Colt's muzzle to lower toward the floor, ready to bring it up again should the need arise.

"Hi was just going to spin him the fanny, Hi'll hadmit," Alfred Higgins replied in what the girl was to come to know was the broad Cockney accent of one born within the sound of Bow Bells in the capital of England. "Only,'e said I should scarper the way Hi'd come in's Monsewer bleeding des Boys Gilbert wasn't noted for being all kind 'n' gentle wiv them's crossed 'im, 'n' the best Hi could hope for would be getting thrashed wivin a ninch of me life afore being throwed art for the dawgs to tear to pieces. So Hi took stoppo's fast's Hi could shinny dahn to the ground. But Hi've *never* forgot what your dad did for me that night 'n' never will."

"I'm going to hold you to that!" Belle warned, knowing de Bois Gilbert was notorious for his savage mistreatment of those who crossed him, and that her father had only been paying the visit to oblige an old friend. "You could be just what I want."

"Hin what way, miss?" Higgins inquired, tearing his eyes

from where the nipples of Belle's well-developed bosom were standing out in bold relief from the flimsy material that snuggled as closely as a second skin about them and the rest of her far-from-straight figure. Then, starting to turn around slowly and with his hands still held clear of his sides, he went on, " 'Cept I'd be obliged if you'd put somefing a bit ficker on. Hit's awful bleeding hard to concentrate wiv you looking like you do.''

"What would your wife and seven children think if they heard you saying such a thing, for shame," Belle inquired, still smiling and continuing to keep a watch on the man in case he should be intending treachery. She placed the revolver on the bed's coverlet so she could gather up and don a more substantial dressing gown. Then she became serious and went on, "Have you heard what happened to Momma and Poppa?''

"No, miss," Higgins replied. Having been told, he responded with what started as a flood of profanity and turned to an apology for its use. "If you're your dad's daughter hand Hi fink you are, Hi'm betting's 'ow you'll be after the bleeders who done him and your mum in.''

"I am," the girl confirmed with a chilling sincerity. "That's why I've come to Richmond, but I can't get any help to do it.''

"You've got whatever 'elp Hi can give you," the Cockney declared. "And, from what you just nah said, Hi fink you've got somefing in mind for me to do.''

"I have," Belle asserted, and explained what she wanted. "Can you do it?''

"Hi'll teach you everyfink Hi can, which's a fair amount hif Hi might make do bold's to say it meself," Higgins promised. "And when you says the word, Hi'll help you pull hit orf no matter who hit'll be done ag'inst.''[2]

---

[2] *Having given a phonetic simulation of the way in which Alfred Higgins spoke throughout this chapter, for the rest of the narrative we will employ normal terms except where the specialized jargon used by the British criminal classes of the period is concerned.*

CHAPTER TEN

You're a Bleeding *Natural*, Miss Boyd

"Here we are, Miss Boyd," Alfred Higgins said quietly yet not without a faint suggestion of a dramatic timbre, looking at the ten-foot-high wall surrounding the grounds of the medium-size mansion that was currently being used as the home and headquarters for General Wilberforce Crumley of the Confederate Army's Quartermaster Corps. "Everything's all gay, but are you *sure* you want to go through with it?"

"I'm sure," the girl replied, her sotto voce tone showing not the slightest hesitancy. During their short acquaintance, she had learned among a number of other things pertaining to what they were planning to do that, in the argot of the criminal circles of London, England, where her companion had been born and raised, the words "all gay" meant there was nobody in the vicinity to see what was intended. "But you don't need to come with me."

"Oh yes I do!" the little Cockney burglar stated, in a manner that implied he would brook no objections. "I've managed to teach you a lot in the time you've been me 'prentice. 'Fact, I've never had a better, but you might still need a bit more know-how afore you can call yourself a regular crib-cracker."

A wry smile twisted at Belle Boyd's lips at the last part of the declaration made by Higgins.

When deciding to try to join the South's Secret Service as part of her quest to find and take revenge upon Alfred Tollinger and George Barmain, the girl had never imagined she would need to employ the method she was intending to use as a means of being brought to their attention.

Nor, Belle told herself, had she envisaged that she would find herself clad in attire similar to that now worn by Higgins when, after having climbed from the street up the outside of the building—acting upon information that he had acquired suggesting there was a quantity of valuable jewelry and money there and the occupant would be absent—he had broken into her room on the second floor of the Sanford Hotel. As an added precaution against being noticed and later recognized, she had her now short-cropped black hair beneath a dark beret and her beautiful face covered with black burned cork.

But then, the girl told herself wryly, she had not anticipated how taking the precaution of learning the tricks of the professional duelist would culminate in her being stripped to the waist in front of a number of men—some of whom would have recognized her without the cloth mask she had on and an alteration in the color and style of her hair—while she was pretending to fight with the Englishwoman called Roxanne Smethers-Fortescue.

In fact, Belle mused, her whole life had changed drastically since the night her parents were murdered and her home burned to the ground.

Even before she had set out upon her mission of revenge, the girl had accepted that such was certain to prove the case.

However, Belle could not avoid having momentary qualms over the means she was intending to use that night under the faint light of a three-quarters moon.

But in spite of her feelings, the girl refused to allow herself to be deterred from the course she had adopted.

Without realizing it, the curvaceously slender Southron beauty was continuing to demonstrate the beginnings of the resolve that would allow her to earn and deserve the sobriquet Rebel Spy.

*   *   *

Belle Boyd could not complain that time had passed slowly, or been wasted, since the night three weeks earlier when she had met Alfred Higgins. As was the case before the destruction of her home and way of life, rising early regardless of how late she had returned or how late she had been up at one of the functions for which Baton Royale Manor had been famous, she had commenced each morning by doing the exercises that helped to keep her in excellent physical condition for whatever arduous tasks might lie ahead. After breakfast, contriving to leave the Sandford Hotel dressed in a manner suitable for the less affluent area of Richmond where she had gone to visit the

Cockney, she had spent her time learning such tricks of his illicit main occupation as she believed might prove of use if she achieved her ambition to be admitted into the Secret Service of the Confederate States.

To prevent the police from thinking he was a gentleman of leisure, as he put it—although not in those exact words—Higgins ran a small, never very busy, and far-from-lucrative shop specializing in the locksmith's trade on the fringes of the better part of town. Except on the rare occasions when the business of the establishment had demanded his attention, he had instructed Belle in the ways access to buildings of various kinds could be gained and things inside opened by using one from a set of what he termed "twirls," but were more generally known as "picklocks" and would eventually be described as "skeleton keys."

Having a keen brain and a possibly inherited manual dexterity, which her parents had encouraged to flourish instead of trying to crush it, as would have been the case with many wealthy Southern families, the girl had quickly acquired an affinity toward manipulating twirls. This had led the little Cockney to exclaim on more than one occasion, "You're a bleeding *natural*, Miss Boyd!" He had claimed that, as a result of his guidance and her own ability, she showed a similar aptitude for other aspects of the housebreaking trade. Furthermore, he had said that if the need arose, he felt sure she would prove capable of effecting an entry at above ground level in the fashion that was his own specialty. In fact, he was so satisfied by her progress that he had agreed without demur to let her put the training into effect in a way of bringing herself to the attention of the people she was seeking.

When the contingency had been discussed, the Cockney had concurred with Belle's opinion that the intended victim would probably prove too embarrassed to take legal action should they be successful, and might even decline to do so on that account if they were caught. If the latter assumption was incorrect, she had promised to do everything in her power to prevent his suffering the consequences regardless of what her own fate might be. She had considered that her father and mother had enough friends—some of whom were holding down positions of importance, if not at the highest level, in

Richmond—who would exert pressure for her to be the recipient of lenient treatment despite having declined to help her make the contact with members of the Secret Service she desired. Nor, due to her determination to take revenge upon the men whom she had seen personally murder her parents and, she had learned, led the mob of drunken rabble that burned down Baton Royale Manor, would she have been deterred if this had not been the case.

With the instructions of the day completed, Belle had returned to her room at the Sandford Hotel to make ready for whatever activity she had selected as offering the best chance of achieving her desire without needing to employ the methods she was contemplating with the aid of the lessons in "crib-cracking" she was receiving from Higgins. She had alternated attending the balls and soirees to which her social standing gave her access without the need for a formal invitation and visiting the less luxurious places where the lower ranks of the Army and, to a lesser extent, Navy spent their off-duty hours in more rowdy and less inhibited fashion than their superiors did openly.

Although the girl had not thought that she had made progress toward her goal at either type of venue as far as she was aware, she had chosen the person she felt was the most suitable—and deserving—subject for the more risky means she was planning to put into effect.

Wilberforce Crumley was large and overweight to the point where it was fortunate that he would never be called upon to see active combat duty, not that such had ever been his intention when choosing to join the Army instead of continuing to run his most lucrative business as a cotton broker along the Mississippi River in Louisiana. From personal experience, Belle knew him to be pompous, overbearing, and not above stooping to sharp practice when granted the opportunity. In fact, she suspected that to be the main reason political pressure had been exerted to have him appointed as a one-star brigadier general without needing to go through the usual military process of gaining practical experience while rising through the lower ranks of officers. It had been thought that this was not needed for him to perform his duties as head of the Quartermaster Corps. She had heard that, probably because he had the backing of men who had spent years in that department of the Union Army prior to coming back to their Southern birth-places when it became obvious that war with the North was unavoidable, he was running things with at least passable efficiency. In spite of this, having found him no more likable in his present capacity than he had been in civilian life during their one meeting since arriving in Richmond, she had felt he would receive less sympathy when it was learned what she was hoping to bring off than would have been the case of a senior officer in a more active command.

Having reached her decision, the girl had not rushed blindly and recklessly into putting her scheme into operation. Once again calling upon the practical knowledge of how to carry out the kind of robbery she envisaged long experience had given Higgins, she had set about learning all she could to help bring her scheme to fruition. Accepting an invitation to an afternoon soiree given by Mrs. Crumley—who possessed most of her husband's outer physical appearance added to an aura of arrant snobbery that had ruled out any misgivings Belle might otherwise have had over the selection of the victim—she had contrived to learn and make an accurate sketch of the building's interior layout and the grounds, which had caused the Cockney to repeat his assertion that she had a natural bent for such matters.

Contriving to meet Mrs. Crumley's white maid off the premises on the day following the soiree, dressed suitably so as to avoid recognition as a guest who had attended it and posing as having a similar and equally unsatisfactory position with the wife of another senior officer, Belle had made her acquaintance and, through her—taking care to avoid arousing any possible jealousy by stating her firm attachment for a sergeant major in a Cavalry regiment—that of a corporal attached to the General's staff with whom she was soon on good terms. It had taken only a short while in their company for the girl to conclude that the pair were ideal for her needs. Neither had the slightest loyalty toward nor liking for their employers, and when away from the house, made no attempt to conceal their hostility.

Hired in the belief that she gave an indication of greater wealth than would have been the case with the more usual

colored servant in that category, the maid was embittered by
having to serve a demanding and far-from-generous mistress.
An old soldier disenchanted by a failure to rise higher in the
ranks, the noncom had a hatred of all officers. This was even
more the case with the one on whose staff he was currently
compelled to serve. Because Crumley was wise to all the tricks
he had hoped to employ, he was unable to augment his pay
by the means he had intended to use.

From the disgruntled pair, with the aid of a few drinks in
a tavern that she had claimed to be purchased with money
acquired from her much-disliked and unsuspecting mistress,
she had gathered information about how the household was
run. The most important factor to have emerged from her point
of view was that Crumley did not have the grounds guarded
in any way at night. Higgins, on being informed of what she
had discovered, offered the equally satisfactory news that, as
neither Crumley nor his wife could abide dogs anywhere near
them, there were none on the premises to make what was
intended more difficult.

Although the girl would have preferred a better-guarded
place, as this would make the successful outcome of her
scheme more impressive, Higgins had stated that they should
be thankful for small mercies and take what was more readily
available than was likely to prove the case elsewhere. Never
one to ignore what she knew to be good advice, despite having
declined to do as Colonel Myles Raines had suggested at the
conclusion of their meeting, Belle had yielded to his greater
experience. He had carried out a personal reconnaissance under the guise of seeking any employment for which his legitimate specialized knowledge would qualify and had returned
from it satisfied that she had done a most excellent piece of
work in discovering all she had to help make the task easier.

Aware that General and Mrs. Crumley were attending a ball
being given by a prominent politician and would not be home
until the early hours of the morning, a situation of which the
girl had discovered the domestic staff would be taking the
fullest advantage, they had set out to put her plan into operation.

* * *

After having made sure that there was still nobody in the vicinity to see what was happening, Alfred Higgins deftly tossed a padded sack, brought along for the purpose of covering the shards of broken glass on the top of the wall, to where he had decided would be the most suitable point at which entry could be gained to the property. Belle Boyd and he were meaning to remove certain items of no especial financial value, as her intention was to arouse interest from the people she was trying to contact by returning them the following day. With the necessary precaution against being cut while going into the grounds taken, he was about to turn, with his back against the wall ready for the next part of the way they were to gain access, when he was forestalled.

Adopting the position for the same purpose before the Cockney could do so, the girl held her cupped hands downward before her with interlocked fingers. Then she braced her shoulders against the wall and gave a cheerful smile accompanied by an upward jerk of her head. Both gestures served to satisfy Higgins that she was not having second thoughts about engaging in what, regardless of its motives, was an illegal action and, considering the identity of the intended victim, might be construed as something even more serious in time of war. He had known male beginners at the house breaking business to be affected in such a fashion when taking part in similar ventures. However, she gave no indication of flinching from her resolve. In fact, her demeanor suggested the opposite. She was determined to go ahead and willing to face whatever consequences might result should they be caught in the act.

Also grinning and making no attempt to comment upon the change in the original arrangements, ensuring that the items suspended from his belt were unlikely to be shaken or slip free, the Cockney placed his right foot in the cupped hands. Combined with the bounding movement he made, the upward thrust from Belle's far-from-puny slender arms raised him until he could hook his arms over and swing himself astride the padded sack. Making sure it was firmly in position beneath him and he had lost nothing from his belt, he bent at the waist and extended his hands. With that done, he braced his legs more tightly on the protective covering and gave a nod.

Moving around, thankful for having decided to fetch a pair of boots intended for savate boxing with the rest of her attire, the girl sprang into the air. Her upraised hands closed on Higgins's wrists, and setting her feet against the wall, she ascended swiftly, helped by the pull his small wiry body was capable of exerting, until she too was sitting on the wall. A quick scrutiny of their surroundings located no cause for concern and the absence of any outcry indicated that they had been spotted, so she turned to first hang and then drop to the garden. A moment later, having a similar lack of difficulty and making no more noise, her smaller companion joined her.

Exchanging looks redolent of satisfaction, the pair advanced stealthily side by side through the decorative bushes and across the lawn, which was now poorly kept by the temporary occupants, or rather by those whose duties it should have been to carry out the gardening duties. They arrived as intended at the right side of the house, still without having been challenged. Not that either was particularly surprised by their invasion of the property having gone unnoticed. Going by what she had seen of them and been told, General and Mrs. Crumley were not the kind of employers to arouse the liking or loyalty of those they hired. Therefore, as she had been informed by the embittered maid would be the case—in the course of their latest seemingly innocuous discussion regarding the less-than-likable qualities of their respective mistresses— the almost total darkness of the building and absence of noise from anywhere inside suggested that the whole of the domestic staff were making the most of the couple's being absent by taking the night off.

"Let's find out whether Fanny was making it up when she said they always leave the French windows of that guest room unfastened," Belle whispered, pointing upward. "It's done so they can sneak in, since they got back late one night and everything was locked up. They had to sleep in the stables, which she said they would have enjoyed if they hadn't needed to make sure they were up before the Crumbs woke up, as they wouldn't have approved of such goings-on between the lower classes."

"They must have a ladder to do it," the Cockney guessed in a similarly low voice, scanning the wall that rose to where a balcony jutted out. "I could shinny up easy on the climb, but I wouldn't think a skivvy wearing a frock could."

"Or even one wearing this what you call clobber," the girl supplemented sotto voce, making a gesture toward her masculine attire.

"Well, I haven't had the time to learn you how to go on the climb, else I bet you could have," Higgins answered, and placed one of the items from where it was suspended on his belt behind his back so it would not be in the way while he was coming over the wall. "And you don't need *their* ladder with this." Wanting to relieve any anxiety the girl might be feeling, he continued, "I got the idea back home from Charlie Peace. You won't heard of him over here, I don't suppose, but he's a real nasty little bleeder. Which's why I steered clear of him as much as possible, although he knows how and where to pull a job."

"I thought you said you always worked alone?" Belle queried, wanting to quell the tension that was growing within her.

"And I allus did," the Cockney confirmed, having told the girl some of the more amusing parts of his career as a criminal in England. "And if I'd ever wanted to go on a job two-handed, it wouldn't've been *him*, 'cause I'm sure he'll come to get topped one of these days."

On being removed and carefully operated by Higgins while the brief whispered conversation was taking place and achieving its purpose where quietening the girl's apprehensions was concerned, what had looked like a bundle of short sticks proved to be a collapsible ladder. Under his manipulations, it extended like lazy tongs upward so the hook at the top passed over the edge of the balcony's decorated protective wall. With it in place, he climbed up swiftly and, on going over, checked the security of the device before signaling for the girl to follow. There was an admiring grin on his face as she made the ascent as swiftly as he had done. Because no suitable height was available at his place of legitimate business, she had been unable to practice going up the device. However, she had claimed she would be able to do so and had justified her confidence.

Having attained the place where they wanted to be, neither Belle nor the Cockney wasted any time in talking. A twist at

the handle of the French windows confirmed the story told by
Fanny: they opened to a push and gave access to the unused
guest room. Making use of the small bull's-eye lamp that Higgins was also carrying on his belt lit but with the cover over
the front, they crossed to the other door and, not unexpectedly,
found that this too was unlocked. Going through brought them
into a wide passage with several other doors; making use of
the information Belle had acquired while paying the visit as a
guest at the soiree, she led the way to one. This proved to be
locked, the illumination emanating from beneath the door provided by a lamp left burning for the benefit of the couple on
their return from the ball, but the skill that the girl had acquired
enabled her to open it with one of the twirls made and presented to her by the Cockney.

"Why does he have his bleeding office up here?" Higgins
inquired, looking around with the aid of his bull's-eye lantern
at what had apparently been converted from a fair-size bedroom into a place where business could be conducted.

"To make more work for the servants, according to
Fanny," Belle replied. "I'm sure we'll find what we need
here."

Examining some of the bulky files and other documents,
the girl selected half a dozen that covered only the most mun-
dane military subjects and placed them into the sack she had
carried tucked in the back of her belt. While she was doing
so, the Cockney was standing at the door through which they
had entered and keeping watch along the passage. Pulling tight
the drawstring, she carried the far-from-valuable or-secret loot
to join her companion.

"Well, that is that," the girl declared. "Now let's get away,
and tomorrow I'll see this gets back to him. Perhaps that will
make them realize I can be of use to the Secret Service."

"If it don't," the irrepressible Cockney replied, "you can
allus start working two-handed with *me*."

CHAPTER ELEVEN

There's No Room In *This* Organization

"You know something, Miss Boyd?" Alfred Higgins said in the low tones they had employed all through the successful robbery they had just committed, as he and the slender, beautiful Southern girl were approaching the point on the rear wall of the house where the padded sack lay across its broken-glass-surmounted top. "I've heard Mrs. Crumb, as you reckon the skivvy 'n' corporal calls her behind her back, has got some pretty good tom, none of it jar neither, and it'd make a nice tickle for us if we start working two-handed."

"That's a thoroughly immoral suggestion to make to a future member of the Confederate States Secret Service, sir," Belle Boyd declared in mock horror. She had learned enough about the argot of London's criminals to be aware that a "nice tickle" referred to a good quantity of loot, "tom" was an abbreviation of tomfoolery and Cockney rhyming slang for jewelry, while "jar" meant the items were made from a stone inferior to diamonds. "Anyway, as soon as he hears what's happened, which he will even though I'll have returned all we're taking away, General Crumb will take precautions against another robbery happening."

"He's just sneaky enough to do it," Higgins admitted with what appeared to be a heartfelt sigh and cast a glance redolent of disappointment at the building. "But, same's I said, it'd've been a bloody nice tickle, just what me mum always wanted me to have when she sent me off at night to go on the climb back home."

"I can always make it worth your whi—!" the girl began.

"Not on your Nellie, Miss Boyd!" the Cockney refused, vehemently and yet with a politeness that might have surprised some of his criminal acquaintances. "Thank you for offering again. But, like what I said before, what your dad done for me that night in des Boys Gilbert's place's all the paying I'll ever need for helping you.''

"Then we might as well take stoppo," Belle suggested, employing another of the terms that had cropped up when she was listening to the anecdotes her companion had told her about his illicit activities before coming to America for reasons he had not disclosed nor had she questioned.

"Blimey, I hope *not*!" Higgins asserted. "That means we have to take our bleeding hook doing a lively, 'cause we've been lumbered 'n' they're after us.''

"Poppa always use to tell me that America and England were two nations divided by a common language," the girl said with a smile, laying down the bundle containing the items she was removing from the headquarters of General Wilberfore Crumley so she could play her part in the scaling of the wall surrounding the property. "And I've come to know just what he meant since meeting you."

"Be fair, miss," the Cockney protested, also grinning and thinking what a great pity he would never have such a partner with whom he would be willing to break his habit and work two-handed. "With all due respect to your dad, it was *us* who invented the bleeding language."

"That's why *we* got rid of you in 'seventy-six," Belle countered, and placed her back against the wall with hands cupped, ready to help her companion with the ascent.

Reaching the top of the wall was accomplished with no greater difficulty than when the pair had come over it on their arrival. Once Higgins was in position, Belle threw the sack containing the documents from Crumley's office to him and he dropped them over the other side. On her joining him, he assisted her in making the descent. Then, to remove the last trace of their illicit visit, he grasped the inner edge of the padded cover and, taking it with him, rolled from his perch. Being skilled as what a later generation would refer to as a cat burglar, a drop of the height he needed to make encumbered with the protective covering was nothing to him. However, as he alighted by the girl and she was picking up the sack, there was a nasty surprise in store for them.

"You did that *real* well!" announced a masculine voice

with a Southern accent having a suggestion of a good education. "Now you can come along with us!"

Leaving their places of concealment and converging swiftly on the pair, the four men who appeared were clad alike in dark-colored civilian clothing—even to their collarless shirts—which in the available light gave no suggestion by its quality and style of their stations in life. All were larger and more powerfully built than the Cockney, but this did not make any of them slow-moving or clumsy on their feet. The only slight consolation Belle could draw—and she assumed Higgins felt the same—was that none were holding weapons or worse badges of office to indicate an official status.

"Scarper, Miss B.!" the Cockney yelled while swiftly discarding the once again folded collapsible ladder and bull's-eye lantern from his belt and, ducking his head, starting to charge at the closest man. "Take *stoppo!*"

"The *hell* I will!" the girl spluttered, and let the sack fall from her fingers.

Although considering the advice to be justified, the sense of responsibility to others that had been instilled into her since childhood would not allow Belle to take it. To have done so would leave the friendly little Englishman who had willingly helped her at the mercy of the approaching quartet. Whoever they might be, that was a situation not to be contemplated or accepted without helping him make the fight he was going to put up so she might be able to escape.

Darting forward even faster than the Cockney, the girl once more blessed the footwear she had on for the ease of movement it permitted. Bending her feet into a half-crouched position without slowing her pace on coming into what she estimated to be the most effective range, she sprang into the air. Straightening the limbs and bending them under her body as she twisted it slightly, she propelled her feet forward with a thrusting motion. Caught in the chest by the soles of the savate boots, the man she had selected as her target went staggering back a few steps. Glancing around at the moment of impact, she found that Higgins had delivered the charge with rather less success: his objective was taller and able to withstand the impact with it failing to achieve its purpose.

Dropping to the ground, Belle saw the man attacked by the Cockney swing a punch that sent him sprawling to the ground in the flaccid way of one stunned by the blow. Then she had troubles of her own. Caught around the arms from the rear, she had them pinned to her sides with a strength against which she knew she could achieve nothing by muscle power alone. Nor did having her feet swung from the ground increase her chances of effecting an escape. Nor, although she used them to fend off the third member of the quartet as he came toward her, was the respite she gained of sufficient length of time for her to try to effect an escape from the bearlike hugging applied by her captor. Then the last of the group came over from an angle where she was unable to reach him. He had taken something from his jacket pocket that felt wet and had a sweet sickly smell as it was clapped onto her face. Although guessing what the liquid must be, as she had occasionally smelled chloroform when helping her mother—who had always kept in touch with the latest medical developments—use it while performing urgent treatment in the absence of a doctor, she tried to hold her breath and struggle. Neither proved to be of any avail, and she felt a blackness descending upon her as she sank into an unconscious state.

*   *   *

"Where am I?" Belle Boyd groaned as sentience returned to her.

"How do you feel?" inquired an unseen speaker with a feminine Southern timbre suggestive of good breeding and education, the voice coming from among the mists that seemed to be surrounding the girl.

"Terrible!" Belle croaked.

"And so you should," the speaker asserted coldly. "Pulling a foolish game like you were. Your momma and poppa would have been ashamed of you."

"Where—?" the girl croaked, thinking the voice seemed vaguely familiar as she began shaking her head and trying to sit up. "What—?"

"Lie still, girl!" the speaker commanded in a less-than-solicitous fashion. "The effects will wear off all the quicker if you do."

Taking the advice, Belle soon found it was valid. As the mists began to clear, she found she was lying on a settee in a luxuriously furnished room. Despite the means employed to bring her there, she was not fastened up in any way. Nor, she slowly became aware, were any of her captors present. However, as a result of having been rendered unconscious by the application of chloroform, she did not believe their absence made her position any more safer. Regardless of who the apparently Southern-born woman with whom she had spoken might be, although her hands and feet were at liberty, she knew that she would be unable to take any kind of positive action in her present enfeebled condition. At last, her vision cleared sufficiently for her to make out even more of her surroundings.

"*You!*" Belle gasped as her gaze came to rest upon the speaker.

"Me," the woman replied.

Staring as if unable to believe the evidence of her eyes, Belle concluded that it was obvious how her mother's cousin had become known as a leading hostess in the society of Washington, D.C., over the past few years.

In her midthirties, Rose Greenhow had strikingly beautiful patrician alabaster features with proud hazel eyes and more than a suggestion of intelligence in their lines. Although the way in which her much longer, immaculately coiffured black tresses made the difference appear more pronounced, she was an inch taller than her niece. Her figure was displayed to its best advantage by a stylish black ball gown with a close-to-daring décolleté. Statuesque in its dimensions, its proudly jutting imposing bosom above a naturally slender waist and richly contoured hips was of the "hourglass" variety so much favored by members of the opposite sex at that period. Everything about her, especially the amount of jewelry glistening in the light of the room from her ears, around her nacreous throat, and on her wrists and fingers, denoted the possession of the most excellent taste.

"But I thought you were in Washington!" Belle said in a puzzled tone.

"I *was*," Rose replied calmly, studying the girl who had always been her favorite niece in a more speculative than amiable fashion. "But I heard Allan Pinkerton was taking a most unhealthy interest in my affairs and considered it was prudent for me to come back home. The more important thing right now is what kind of game you've been playing for the past few weeks.''

"Game?" Belle repeated, then a remembrance of whom she had been with forced her to attain a sitting position. Anxiety helped her to fend off the dizziness caused by the sudden movement, and she demanded rather than asked, "Where is Alfred Higgins?"

"Is that the little locksmith—and far more, I should imagine—who you've been spending so much time with recently?" Rose inquired.

"It is," the girl confirmed. "And if he's been hurt—!"

"He hasn't," the beautiful Southron woman stated in a reassuring tone. "But it took all Captain Dartagnan's considerable persuasive powers to convince him *you* had not been harmed, nor would be."

"Where is he now?" Belle insisted.

"In the kitchen, drinking whiskey and regaling my friends with what I suspect are ribald tales of his criminal exploits in England," Rose said soothingly. "He's not harmed, nor will he be. However, after Alex had persuaded him to return your—loot, shall we call it?—and conceal all traces of what you had done, he insisted upon being brought here to make certain you are all right."

"Then he may get his nice tickle after all," the girl said with a smile.

"I beg your pardon?" the woman asked in genuine puzzlement, lacking the knowledge her niece had acquired about the argot of criminals in London.

"It's a private joke, *Aunt* Rose," Belle answered, knowing the reference to their relationship had never been popular with the Southron beauty on the grounds that it made her appear old.

"What you've been doing since you arrived in Richmond *hasn't* been a joke," Rose warned, and raised a hand before the girl could speak. "Oh, I know what you've been trying to do and why you've played that game tonight. Well, you have achieved your intention."

"You mean—!"

"You've found the South's Secret Service, or rather a part of it, at least."

"Are you a member of it?"

"I am and have been for some considerable time."

"Then why didn't you—?"

"Why didn't I come straight over to the Sandford and visit to tell you?" Rose finished for the girl. "I've only been back for a day, and I meant to do so after having heard all you've been getting up to."

"Do you mean that—" Belle began, but once again words failed her.

"You've been kept under observation ever since it came to the attention of our people that you were behaving the way you were," Rose confirmed, nodding her head gracefully and smiling at the confusion being shown by her generally composed and self-possessed niece. "At first it was suspected you might be a Yankee spy, then Colonel Raines told Alex who you were and why you were trying to meet members of the Secret Service." She lost all traces of levity as a thought struck her, and she continued in a contrite fashion, "Let me offer my condolences over the death of your parents, dear, and please forgive me for not having done so immediately."

"No apologies are necessary, *Rose*," Belle stated, and hoped not saying "Aunt" would show she harbored no ill feeling over the omission. "Then I don't need to tell you why I wanted to meet and, if I could, join the Secret Service."

"You don't," the beautiful woman asserted, and all the kindliness left her face. She stiffened as if preparing herself for an unpleasant yet necessary task and went on, "But you can get one thing into your head right now. There's no room in this organization for a vengeance seeker. Don't deny it, Belle, you wouldn't be Electra and Vincent Boyd's daughter if you didn't want to do something to avenge their death. The thing is, although everything you've done since coming to Richmond—even that escapade tonight—had made us sure that you can be of use to us, you *can't* use the Secret Service for your personal ends."

"I won't," Belle promised without hesitation, realizing that there was no other way she would gain the acceptance she wanted—even more now that she had discovered her favorite aunt's involvement in the organization she had been seeking. "And you have my *word*, as Electra and Vincent Boyd's daughter, on it."

"That's good enough for me," Rose affirmed. "From tonight you can count yourself a member of the Confederate States Secret Service. However, capable and determined as you've shown yourself to be, there are still things you have to learn before we will let you go on any assignments. And, Belle, while none of us will mind if you deal with Tollinger and Barmain as they deserve should your paths cross, you must *never* under *any* circumstances turn aside from your assigned duty to do it. Is that understood?"

"It *is*!" the girl declared. "Now, as he's been such a good friend and helpful to me, can I go and see Alfred?"

"You can, after you've washed that black stuff off your face," Rose confirmed. "And I'll come with you. I'm rather keen to hear the ending of the story he stopped telling about how he was compelled to respond when a titled lady at a house he was robbing mistook him in the darkness for her husband and insisted—Well, let's go and see if we can persuade him to fill in the details he was tactful and, I consider, unsporting enough to leave untold when he became aware that I was listening."

Rising to carry out her aunt's instructions with regard to her appearance, Belle felt a sense of elation. Despite the restriction on the freedom to hunt for the murders of her parents that she had willingly agreed to on realizing why they had been imposed, she decided she would do anything possible to justify the faith Rose was putting in her, and after whatever additional training she was to be given, she meant to do everything she could to be a very useful Rebel spy.

PART TWO

THE BEGINNING

I Think She May Have Recognized Me

"Good evening, sir," boomed the elderly-looking and well-dressed man who had accompanied Belle Boyd into the mansion in Atlanta, Georgia, that had been converted to a luxurious gambling house. "My name is Culpepper, *Colonel* Ebediah F. Culpepper the Third. Retired, of course. *They* say I'm too old for duty, sir. Well, I'll show them." While his left hand tapped the metal ferrule of the silver-topped polished ebony cane in his left hand on the floor as if to emphasize the point he was making, he slapped where the inside breast of his white cutaway jacket bulged with his right palm and went on just as flamboyantly, "I trust, sir, you have liberal funds to meet the winnings I shall have to be used to set up my *niéce* in the manner she deserves?"

It was highly unlikely that anybody who had known the beautiful, willowy girl when she was living happily at Baton Royale Manor would have recognized her at that moment. She was dressed and behaving in the manner required by her pose of being the kind of fluttery, featherbrained, and generally less-than-competent-at-anything Southron maiden already often portrayed on the stage and met in real life often enough to give credence to the character. She had so ably created the guise for her first assignment as a member of the Confederate States Secret Service.

Three months had elapsed since Belle had achieved her purpose by having been inducted into the service of the organization she had sought to locate by employing the unconventional methods that brought her to its member's attention. Although being related to Rose Greenhow, who she had discovered was high in its hierarchy, she was aware that it was solely her own efforts and willingness to learn whatever was required of her that had allowed her to get as far as she had. What was more, on learning how her aunt had been able to

reach Richmond, she had discovered something of the dedication that would be expected from her if she was to succeed
as a Rebel spy.

Finding that the attentions of Allan Pinkerton, who she
claimed to be the most efficient member of the Union's Secret
Service, had made Washington, D.C., too hot for safety and
also having acquired intelligence of vital importance that must
be delivered to her superiors with a minimum of delay, Rose
had contrived with the help of another lady with Southern
sympathies, but who was unable to travel from the North for
family reasons, to escape. When telling Belle of the means
employed, sounding a trifle defiant and perhaps even a little
conscience-stricken, the beautiful black-haired woman had
stated that she would not have permitted the sacrifice of liberty
if the intelligence she had acquired had not been a matter of
highest importance.

Being a realist, the girl had accepted that she might be
compelled to reach similar unpleasant decisions in the work
that lay ahead and hoped she would have the strength of will
to behave in the same fashion.

There was one thing of which Belle felt confident. Should
she fail in her duties, it would not be because of a lack of
training. In fact, even more than while she was carrying out
the program that led to her being brought to the attention of
Captain Alexandre Dartagnan, the tall, debonair and handsome
French Creole—who could prove to be descended from the
famous Gascon swordsman of that name—almost every day
had been fully occupied by something that would offer her a
greater chance of survival or prove of use for the duties she
was to perform.

The skills that Belle had acquired from Alfred Higgins were
improved under his still-willing guidance, with him expressing
such admiration for the way they had been followed undetected by him to their burglary that he had offered his services
to the organization. Having seen proof of his abilities by the
way in which he had helped the girl carry out the robbery and
then return the loot—chosen so carefully by her as being em-
barrassing to the loser rather than of military importance or
secrecy—with such dexterity and care that General Wilber-

force Crumley never learned its temporary removal had taken place, this was accepted without reservations.

Instructed by Rose, who was an expert in the subject, as had been proved by the way her return to Richmond had been effected, the girl had improved her already latent ability at creating different characters by using disguises and had been supplied with several things—including the start of a collection of realistic-looking wigs—to give greater credence to whatever persona she adopted. She had become adept at using the code employing a substitution of letters by numbers with which messages could be passed.[1] Although competent in the use of savate, she had learned from Dartagnan to employ methods of attack that would result in an immediate disqualification if applied during a formal sporting contest. He had told her with Gallic humor that, instead of making the spectacular leaping high kick to the chest when trying to go to Higgins's assistance, she would have achieved far better results by delivering a more potent kick to somewhere he described as being "between neck and knee" and was followed by a demonstration that indicated the point on the masculine anatomy he had in mind.

Much to Belle's satisfaction, as they were subjects generally regarded as being male-only accomplishments—especially by members of her class, especially in the Southern states—

---

[1] *The code that was currently in use was based on the song most used by the Union as a comic counter to the South's "Dixie."*

> *Yankee doodle came to town riding on a pony,*
> *He stuck a feather in his cap and called it macaroni*

Y	A	N	K	E	D	O	L	C	M	T	W	R	I	G	P	H	S	U	F	B	J	Q	V	X	Z
1	2	3	4	5	6	7	8	9	10	11	12	13	14	15	16	17	18	19	20	21	22	23	24	25	26
A	B	C	D	E	F	G	H	I	J	K	L	M	N	O	P	Q	R	S	T	U	V	W	X	Y	Z
9	6	5	20	15	17	14	22	4	8	10	3	7	16	23	13	18	11	18	11	19	24	12	25	1	26

There was no punctuation and the recipient had to use judgment in forming the words of the actual message. Nevertheless, we are informed that there were very few errors on this account.

[1a] *The very patriotic and rousing words put to Daniel D. Emmett's minstrel song, "Dixie" by General Albert Pike, C.S.A., are recorded in* TO ARMS! TO ARMS! IN DIXIE!

and of which she suspected her aunt did not entirely approve despite appreciating how useful having them was likely to be, there had been fields in which it was considered she already possessed a sufficiency of competence. Because of the training she had received at her father's instigation, she had a superlative ability at riding a horse sidesaddle or astride across the most difficult terrain, a skill that was to serve her so well in her career.

Furthermore, having demonstrated it in practice, the girl's ability in the use of firearms of various kinds had received praise. On having put to the test her ability at fighting, as opposed to formally fencing, Dartagnan, being an acknowledged master at both, had claimed that the lessons learned from Captain Anatol de-Farge had been so comprehensive in their scope that there was nothing further he could teach her. The devices for self-protection supplied by the gambler had met with the approval of everybody to whom they were shown, as did the modification she had had made to her skirts at his suggestion. To the former implements, she had added the kind of most effective concealed and disguised weapon that her aunt possessed, and one of them would be an important factor in her later survival. It was claimed that the instructions in detecting and even using some of the methods employed by dishonest professional gamblers, given by an old friend of her family to add to her other unconventional accomplishments, might serve another useful purpose when she commenced her duties.

As time went by and she realized she was gaining an ever-growing satisfaction over the way her training was progressing, Belle had begun to become impatient to commence active duties. Although she never forgot her desire to take a justifiable revenge upon Alfred Tollinger and George Barmain for the murder of her parents—Rose having contrived to learn that they had joined other "liberals" in a section of the Yankee Secret Service that was less efficient than the branch run by Allan Pinkerton without as yet finding out where they might be serving—she had accepted that they were probably beyond her reach in the line of duty. What was more, she never allowed herself to forget the promise she had given on her word of honor to her aunt on the night they met, and continually swore to herself she would never turn aside from her duty should she learn where she could find them.

The chance for the girl to be sent into what her companions referred to as "the field" came as the result of complaints from their superiors being received by Rose Greenhow in a coded message. There was a serious leakage of information taking place in Atlanta, and Belle was sent with Dartagnan to help try to locate, then stamp out, the source. At her suggestion, made because Higgins had said his specialized services might prove useful and asked her to make it, he was included in the small party. On arrival and after establishing contact, they had found that the local agents had made considerable progress in the matter, but felt their assistance would be of little use in bringing the matter to a conclusion.

As a result of the investigations carried out on the spot, it had been ascertained that the first part of the problem was almost certainly the result of a small number of Army and Navy officers—not all of whom were young and of junior rank—and others in positions allowing access to items that the North would find of use, being regular participants in the games of chance offered at a high-class gambling house in the city. Several were known to have sustained heavy losses and lacked the financial means to settle their debts, yet they had not appeared to be pressed by the owners to do so. In fact, there had been rumors that some had had the liabilities discounted supposedly on grounds of loyalty to the Southern cause. While such a contingency was possible, the local operative had stated that the owners of the gambling house would be most unlikely to show generosity in such a fashion, as to do so would establish what they were almost certain to regard as a dangerous precedent.

Wanting the matter investigated, Colonel Charles Jeremiah Mason, the head of the Secret Service in Atlanta, had suggested that the matter be handled by the visitors from Richmond, since they were strangers in the town and less likely to arouse suspicion than any of his men, all of whom—with one exception—had been residents for some time and had never shown any interest in gambling, even before taking up their duties.

On being introduced to the exception, Belle had been de-

lighted to find that he was Joseph Brambile, who in addition
to being a successful professional gambler was an old friend
of her family. Without waiting to be told of the accomplishments she had added since their last meeting, as he had heard
what happened to her parents, he guessed what had motivated
her to join the Secret Service. Therefore, he had suggested a
means by which proof might be obtained about the honesty of
the gambling house if nothing more positive.

"Ole Dixie," as the Colonel was cheerfully and respect-
fully referred to behind his back by his juniors on account of
his being a descendant of one of the men who surveyed what
had already become known as the Mason-Dixon line and accepted as separating the Southern "slave" and Northern
"free" states, had agreed that the proof would at least allow
the establishment to be closed and its owners and employees
to be run out of town. However, it was apparent to Belle from
the way he had looked briefly in her direction that—due to his
upbringing as a Southern gentleman—he had been far from
enamored of making use of her services in the capacity that
was suggested. However, Brambile had insisted that she was
a most essential part of the deception he was planning, and
Dartagnan had rallied to her support by declaring that there
was no woman more capable of self-protection should the need
for this arise. Accepting both points, Mason had given what
was clearly an acceptance filled with unspoken misgivings.

Because the matter was regarded as being of the greatest
urgency, no time had been wasted in putting the plan proposed
by Brambile into effect. To avoid being recognized, although
he had not been even close to Atlanta in several years, he had
adopted the attire of a well-to-do plantation owner older than
Brambile himself. For her part, Belle had donned a blond wig
of a suitable style to go with the expensive dress and other
accoutrements—including the protective devices from de-
Farge and a fancy parasol of a style copied in every respect
from one in the possession of her aunt—to add credence to
the character in which she had been introduced: his less-than-
bright and insipidly garrulous, albeit trimly curvaceous and
beautiful companion whom he claimed to be his niece but who
gave the impression of qualifying more accurately as his mistress.

* * *

"Yes, Colonel," Martin Jacques confirmed with the suggestion of bonhomie he always exuded so convincingly when addressing men he knew to be very wealthy and less-than-successful gamblers. Big, burly, with features just short of ugly, he was excellently and expensively dressed in a manner that gave no indication of how he earned his living. He glanced quickly to where his partner, David Hunt—whose lean and gaunt physique was clad in a similar fashion—stood close by listening to what was said while studying the "blonde" in a frankly lascivious manner. "We most certainly *do*, and it is always our pleasure to see it go to a gentleman of distinction like yourself."

"There, Maggie-child," Joseph Brambile boomed in the manner of speech he knew the man he was impersonating invariably used. "I told you we'd come to the right place."

"That you did, Third-honey," Belle Boyd asserted, giving her companion's left arm a squeeze suggestive of affection, in keeping with the character she wanted to establish for "Magnolia Beauregard," the name she had chosen to use and would often use in the future as being indicative of her birth and background. "But then, you're *always* right about *everything*, I do declare."

"What will your pleasure be, Colonel?" Jacques inquired, and waved a fat hand in a leisurely fashion around the big room. "As you can see, we offer a variety of games of chance, and although I say it myself, you won't find any better served nor more honest no matter where you go."

"If I doubted that, sir," the disguised gambler replied with the same feisty bombast, "I would not have brought my niece here in the first place. By the way, allow me to present her. This is Miss Magnolia Beauregard."

"Proud to make your acquaintance, ma'am," the bulky man said formally, with a bow that was deeper than required by convention.

"*Enchanté, m'sieur,*" Belle responded in poorer French than she would normally have employed, while giving a curtsy that allowed Hunt an opportunity that he took the most advantage of to see down into the daring décolleté of her white crinoline gown's bodice. "Third-honey does so *love* to gamble, and I enjoy him doing it."

"Perhaps you would care for a libation while you are making your choice, Colonel?" Jacques suggested, drawing the intended conclusion that Magnolia Beauregard found the participation in gambling served to stir her elderly keeper sexually. "And you, of course, Mam'zelle Beauregard?"

"Can I have some champagne, Third-honey?" Belle cooed. "You know how I dearly *love* what it does to m—the way the bubbles tickle my nose!"

"I certainly *do* and you most certainly *may*," Brambile authorized, also keeping the impression that there was a special significance in the way the first part of the explanation was worded before being altered to something more innocuous. "I'll take a bourbon, sir, while I'm looking around and deciding at which game I will do my winning from you."

"How do you think it's going, Third-honey?" Belle inquired, just loudly enough for Brambile alone to hear, after they had accepted the drinks that were brought by a colored waiter in response to a signal and order from Jacques and they had started to walk slowly across the room.

"What a name you've picked, Maggie-child," the gambler replied no more loudly, pleased and amused by the way in which the girl was making it appear that she was cooing sweet nothings into his ear. "But everything's going along quite satisfactorily so far. The fat feller's obviously heard of Colonel Ebediah F. Culpepper, which I expected to be the case, but hasn't made his acquaintance face-to-face."

"That could have been difficult."

"It could, although I calculated the odds to be in our favor against its having happened. Even if it did, unless they had been on close terms, I was confident I look and sound enough like the good Colonel for him to assume it was only the passage of time which caused any minor discrepancies."

At first, although the girl thought the surroundings were even more opulent than those of Captain Anatol de-Farge—which was understandable, as Baton Rouge was a smaller town than Atlanta—neither paid any particular attention at that moment to the various games of chance that were taking place. Rather, they subjected the people who were present to their scrutiny. The staff were well-dressed and, except for the half a dozen large men who loafed around without doing any kind of work or participating in the games, appeared courteously efficient.

The players were mostly military or naval officers of differing ranks and civilians whose attire implied affluent circumstances. However, there were a few women present. These were alike in being well-dressed and bejeweled. Belle was just wondering which of them were employed by the house. She was just about concluding that she could not tell if this was the case, or they were there either as companions brought by the players or even as participants at the games in their own behalf when she received something of a surprise. It took all her willpower to prevent her perturbation from becoming apparent.

Standing at the faro bank table, which was doing the most business and appeared to have the highest stakes, clad and jeweled as well as any other woman present, was the curvaceously close-to-buxom and attractive English redhead who called herself Roxanne Fortescue-Smethers!

For a moment Belle's eyes locked with those of the redhead.

Then Roxanne looked away and gave her attention to the man by her side.

"What's wrong, B—Maggie-child?" Brambile asked sotto voce, making the alteration to the name he had meant to say even though he was not likely to be overheard. "You look as if you've seen a ghost!"

"Is it *that* obvious?" the girl asked, having felt sure she had just managed to prevent her surprise from showing on her face.

"Only to somebody who knows you as well as I do. So what is it?"

"I've seen somebody I know and I think she may have recognized me."

"Hm!" Brambile breathed noncommittally, and although there was no difference in his face or manner, Belle sensed an air of controlled tension. "Is she a friend, or going by the way you looked likely to prove an enemy?"

"More of an acquaintance," the girl admitted, thinking of

the night she and the redhead put on what they turned into only a pretense at fighting. Then she gave a shrug and went on, ''Well she hasn't done anything yet and I may be wrong about her recognizing me, so we may as well see if we can do what we came here for.''

CHAPTER TWO

I Do Believe We're Being *Cheated*!

"I don't know about you, but I believe we should steer clear of her for the time being," Joseph Brambile decided sotto voce, glancing at the attractive redheaded woman whom his companion contrived to indicate while prattling on in a louder tone about the way in which the bubbles from the glass of champagne she had been given were tickling her nose. "Let her make the first move, if there is going to be one."

"I agree," Belle Boyd answered, dropping her voice and giving the appearance of nibbling at the gambler's ear in a flirtatious fashion. "But I hope there won't be one that could interfere with our plans, because I rather got to *like* her."

"Come, Maggie-dear!" Brambile boomed rather than just said, as befitted his well-performed impersonation of Colonel Ebediah F. Culpepper the Third, wondering how the acquaintanceship had occurred, as the curvaceously close-to-buxom redhead—regardless of being expensively dressed and bejeweled—did not strike him as belonging to the social circles in which his companion mingled before the murder of her parents. In fact, she struck him as being a financially successful "lady of the night" indulging in a passion for gambling while possibly hoping to be brought into contact with a wealthy customer. Another solution could be that she was a shill for the house, intended to encourage others to bet on various games, but he did not consider this likely or she would have found some way of warning her employers that Belle and he were not what they were pretending to be. He extricated himself from the girl's arm and placed his empty glass on the tray of a passing colored servant, who had paused to accept the one she had contrived to drain while engaging in the low-spoken, flirtatious, yet seemingly innocuous conversation. "Let us away and see whereabouts we shall acquire the wherewithal for the little present I promised you."

Although scrupulously honest himself, Brambile had considered it imperative that he acquire very thorough information
about the methods employed by professional cheats. Having
faith in his ability where such things were concerned, he was
convinced that he could detect any malpractices that were being employed by the staff of the gambling house operated by
Martin Jacques and David Hunt. As he had told Colonel
Charles Jeremiah Mason when summoned to help discover
whether the suspicions regarding the way in which the gambling house was being used to help the Union's cause were
correct, he had never heard of the pair but believed he might
be able to provide proof if any existed. He had not anticipated
being given the assistance of the beautiful and clearly most
competent daughter of his old friends Electra and Vincent
Boyd, but had soon become satisfied that her presence would
be an asset. What was more, going by all he had heard when
she was not present from Captain Alexandre Dartagnan and
the little Cockney criminal who clearly revered her, he felt
sure she would be far from a burden in need of his protection
if trouble should occur.

Memories of how Belle had been prominent in the amateur
theatricals often forming part of the entertainment at Baton
Royale Manor when he was visiting there and stood out from
most of the other performers by virtue of her ability to inject
every role she was assigned with realism, the gambler had felt
sure she would prove beneficial to him at the gambling house,
and that was the reason he had been adamant in the face of
Ole Dixie's opposition. Nor had he had any reason to regret
the choice since they arrived. As they started to walk across
the big room toward a table where draw poker was being
played, watching the way she continued to behave in the manner of somebody with the personality she was giving to her
alter ego Magnolia Beauregard, he felt there were professional
actresses as well as female participants in confidence tricks
and others seeking to lure gullible males by a pretense of featherbrained irresponsibility who could not have bettered her performance.

Feeling certain that there would be nothing he could
achieve at any of the tables where poker was the game, Brambile took advantage of the way in which the girl's deliberately

frivolous chatter was continued to such effect that even the
younger players—who at other times would probably have
shown an interest in her all too openly flaunted physical attributes—directed glances of annoyance her way. Acting in
accordance with the instructions she had received, her declaration that she would sit next to him so she could bring him
good fortune by kissing the cards he was dealt—which he had
told her was anathema to all dedicated aficionados of the game
when carried out by kibitzing members of her sex—aroused
the hostility to a point where he used it as an excuse for them
to move on with a gesture of what appeared to be apology for
her conduct from him.

While Belle and Brambile continued the circuit of the various games of chance being played, in addition to maintaining
the convincing rendering of her part as his far-less-than-
intelligent mistress, she kept darting surreptitious glances at the
red-haired woman she knew as Roxanne Fortescue-Smethers,
who gave the appearance of not being accompanied by anybody
else. What the girl noticed did nothing to relieve her concern
over what the outcome of the chance encounter might be. On
more than one occasion, she found that she was receiving a similar covert scrutiny that was brought to an end as soon as her
own gaze was detected. Deciding that the wisest thing for her to
do was to follow the suggestion from her companion, she put
the matter from her mind and concentrated upon the work they
were in the gambling house to do.

When explaining to Belle what the plan was, because of
his expert reading of the possible situation, Brambile had said
that he considered his best chance of detecting any malpractices would be at one of the games supervised for the house
by a banker. Therefore, knowing it would be expected of Colonel Culpepper, he had done no more than look briefly at the
poker games, even though they were being controlled by a
dealer who took a percentage of each pot for the running expenses instead of allowing the handling of the cards to be done
by the players. Because of this, his knowledge of how dishonest gambling houses operated caused him to assume that there
would be no need of cheating tactics for a continuous profit
to be made that more than covered the financial outlay involved, since no layout upon which various bets could be made

was required and only one man was needed to run things. Furthermore, even if there were other employees present in the guise of players, he knew exposing them would not be so useful for his purposes as elsewhere.

Having similar feelings where the few games of whist were being engaged upon by elderly men—most of whom were senior officers in the Army and Navy—the gambler had had no intention of participating. Therefore, when he was offered a place by a ruddy-faced admiral of advanced years and the remaining players gave indications of expecting him to accept it, Belle provided him with an excuse to decline by producing what in theatrical terms was a piece of brilliant ad-libbing.

"Why, you go right ahead, Third-honey," the girl said, and waved her right hand languidly toward where a number of younger men, civilian and military, were noisily playing a less demanding type of game. "I'll just go and *entertain* myself over there at the birdcage."

"Thank you for your offer, sir," Brambile said, showing no sign of the delight he felt over the response from Belle. Rather, he darted a frown redolent of annoyance from her to the young players and back before continuing, "And my apologies for declining, gentlemen, but my inclinations are directed elsewhere tonight."

"Did I do the right thing?" the girl inquired in another of the whispers disguised as flirtatious behavior while walking away, followed by knowing glances and winks on the part of the men at the whist table that implied the required inferences behind the refusal were being drawn.

"You know you did, you little minx," the gambler growled, still continuing the pretense of being annoyed over her hint at being willing—even eager—to spend time in company younger than he. "So stop fishing for compliments and keep keeping your eye on your red-haired friend."

"I wish I could work out what she's here for, because I'm certain it isn't just out of a love for gambling, and although she's alone as far as I can see, she looks far better off than I would expect her to be," Belle said in the low voice, then raised it to a point where it could be heard by everybody close by and even farther away. "When are *we* going to start playing, Third-honey?" She paused before going on archly, "At *gambling*, I mean, of course. And I don't mean at one of those stuffy games where li'l ole me can't join in.''

Still concealing his amusement and satisfaction over the way in which the girl was playing her part with such skill, Brambile did not bother to show any more interest in the four tables given over to pinochle. He knew there were ways of cheating at both this game and whist, but discounted the possibility of any being employed on the same general grounds that caused him to dismiss the games of poker. In fact, he believed he would achieve his purpose by concentrating on the two kinds of card games involving the use of a bank controlled by members of the gambling house's staff.

Although the gambler knew there had been no justification for the apparent concern he had shown over the supposed interest ''Magnolia'' had displayed in the game frequented by the rowdy younger element, this had not caused him to rule it out. Cheating by loading the three dice that were caused to turn over and over in the rotating wire cage was sometimes practiced at chuck-a-luck. However, the results that accrued could only be attained over a long period, and there was always the danger that more astute players would notice and take advantage of how certain numbers kept showing up more frequently than others by placing bets accordingly. With that in mind, knowing Jacques and Hunt would in all probability follow the example of those who ran most other dishonest gambling houses—by putting their reliance solely on the most favorable percentages offered by the incorrect odds given for the various types of wagers—it was to the bank-operated card games that he intended to devote his attention. Having already made his selection, he guided Belle toward the one upon which he intended to concentrate.

A preference for faro rather than a lack of knowledge where chemin de fer—which had been imported from Europe—was concerned caused the gambler to select the table at which the basically American game was being played for the highest stakes. Following him, regardless of her ''Magnolia'' behavior remaining in full flower by declaring loudly that she never could stand that foreign game because of all the ciphering of numbers it required, Belle felt a sensation of anticipation and not a little excitement rising as she realized that they were

approaching a spot where he hoped to obtain evidence upon
which he could make his move. Without deserting her pose
for a moment, she met another brief glance from Roxanne
without showing the slightest indication of awareness that it
was being made. Being vacated by two naval lieutenants
whose expressions suggested they were leaving in a worse
financial condition than when they had started to play, the
place to which her companion guided her was at the opposite
end of the long table where the redhead was now sitting.

Because her mother and father had never been addicts of
gambling, only mingling with a few people such as Brambile
who were, and then never indulging in games of chance, the
girl had only a basic idea of how faro was played.[1] Not that
she had expected she would have any need to do so at more
than the level of a novice as featherbrained as she was pur-
porting to be. Brambile had told her what part she was to play,
and because of their simplicity, she felt certain she could carry
out his instructions. However, she had also decided to add an
embellishment as an experiment with one of the devices given
to her by Captain Anatol de-Farge. The ruse she intended to
employ was a test of whether the means she had devised for
its use would be practical under actual conditions.

On sitting down and studying the way in which the game
was being conducted with the eye of a professional well-versed
in such matters, Brambile concluded that Jacques and Hunt
had either been fortunate not to have had anybody else as
knowledgeable as himself among their patrons or succeeded
in keeping silent those who were. He only needed one glance
at the box from which the cards were being passed out to know
he was not in an honest game. Just large enough to hold a full
deck of cards, it had a slot in front to allow the dealing of
individual cards—apparently one at a time—by a push through
a small hole in the top that permitted only a small portion of
the back of the one uppermost to be seen. While this ruled out
the use of marked cards, as the secret symbols that were
needed for the purposes of identification of suit and denomi-

---

[1] *An admittedly brief description of how the game of faro was played is
given in* RANGELAND HERCULES.

nation could not have been seen, he knew they were unnecessary under the circumstances.

From experience acquired elsewhere, the gambler was aware that such open and aboveboard manipulation was not the purpose of the box in use at the table. There was only a hole large enough for a finger to enter. Furthermore, having examined a number of similarly manufactured devices, he was aware that its operation was achieved by pressure on a tiny unnoticeable button that narrowed or widened the slot so either one or two cards at a time could be emitted.

The employment of such a "brace" or "screw" box, as the device was known, could be achieved only by using "Sand Tell" or similarly prepared cards wherein the higher denominations were roughened a trifle on the faces and the lower at the back. When both surfaces that were "sanded" came into flush contact, they could easily be caused to stick together by pressure on the uppermost. Therefore, if the dealer did not want a high or a low denomination to appear next, he only needed to press on the top card and the different widths of the slot allowed him to send out one or two as was required. Since other varieties of bets were available, the use of the contraption did not mean the patrons had no chance of winning. On the other hand, once again the percentages in favor of the house ensured that it received a consistent level of advantage that was enhanced by the cheating being carried out.

By placing his bets on the layout in a seemingly erratic fashion, Brambile ensured that he maintained steady losses augmented by doubling the amount wagered each time the bet failed. At his side, Belle was playing her part as the inept "Magnolia" with a skill he admired, and she too was a winner only on rare occasions. He was amused and impressed by the way in which she conducted a test that she had never mentioned to him. They were seated next to the dealing box, and when he was asked after joining the game to shuffle the deck about to be put into use, she contrived to scan the backs of the cards he let slide from his seemingly clumsy hands through the magnifying lens at the front of the locket she was wearing. She did this in such a fashion that even a person suspicious of her intentions might not have noticed she had opened the

front before manipulating the device in a seemingly casual
fashion. However, as there were no secret indications of denomination and suit, he knew her attempts were in vain.

After about ten minutes of play, during which she displayed
a well-simulated growing annoyance at consistently being a
loser, Belle received the signal from Brambile that told her she
must commence the next part of the scheme.

"Third-honey!" the girl screeched on receiving the brief
nod of the head from the gambler that informed her she was
required to carry on with the scheme, at the same time thrusting back her chair and coming to her feet. As she intended,
her voice was pitched so it would carry to every corner of the
big room. "I do believe we're being *cheated*!"

Instantly, a silence that could almost be felt descended over
the people present.

CHAPTER THREE

Calm Yourselves, Ladies and Gentlemen!

I t was obvious from the response to the declaration by Belle Boyd that the two owners of the gambling house and their staff were prepared to deal with the kind of situation her words threatened to provoke.

However, although the girl was not yet aware of the fact, her misgivings over the presence of Roxanne Fortescue-Smethers were needless.

In fact, the red-haired Englishwoman was about to prove herself a useful ally.

At the other end of the long faro table, Roxanne was feeling a surge of relief as she watched what was happening. Keeping the promise he had made when agreeing to supply the instruction, Captain Anatol de-Farge had not told her or anybody else why Belle had been receiving lessons in the less-than-fair handling of a sword. Thinking about the matter, the redhead had concluded that it had something to do with the girl intending to avenge the murder of her parents. While it had come as a surprise to see Belle arrive at the gambling house dressed and behaving in such an untypical fashion, Roxanne had felt the reason might prove beneficial to the purpose for which she had come.

A matter of family honor affecting her employer, for whom she had such a great liking and respect that she had not hesitated before agreeing when asked to render the assistance he requested, was responsible for the redhead's being present. Phillipe de-Farge was among those officers who had transferred allegiance at the approach of open hostilities between the Southern and Northern states by going to serve as a lieutenant in the Army of what soon became called the Johnny Rebs. Posted to the staff of the commanding general in Atlanta, he had fallen so deeply into debt as a result of playing various games of chance at the gambling house operated by Martin Jacques and David Hunt that he had committed suicide.

Having read the letter the young lieutenant wrote to his parents just before shooting himself, Anatol de-Farge had been convinced there was more than just the repayment of the money. He had always had a liking for Phillipe, and being aware of the pride the other had always shown for the military career, he had concluded that the deed was done to avoid being compelled to deliver secrets that would be detrimental to the Confederate States' cause. Being just as loyal to the South, he had sworn he would find out whether the supposition was correct. Furthermore, the family's French-Creole code of honor—to which Anatol adhered as strictly as any of the others, regardless of his way of life—demanded that some action be taken to lessen the stigma of suicide. Therefore, he had been determined to find out the truth of the matter and take revenge on the pair whether his suppositions proved correct or the debt had been incurred as a result of cheating.

As far as Anatol de-Farge knew, his path had never crossed that of either Jacques or Hunt. However, he was aware that men of the kind he suspected them to be frequently changed their names. Even if this did not apply, he had been successful in one affair of honor that aroused much interest and was brought to public attention during an earlier visit to Atlanta. Therefore, because he was sufficiently well known as a gambler and a duelist to make it unlikely he could pass unrecognized at the gambling house, and in all probability his connection with his cousin would be remembered.

With those contingencies in mind, de-Farge had brought Roxanne—the one of his female employees he considered the most intelligent, very trustworthy because of the close relationship that had developed between them, and possessed of the courage necessary for doing what was required—with him to Atlanta. Staying with friends he knew could be relied on not to let his presence in the city become known, he had had the redhead dress in a suitable fashion and provided sufficient money to aid her pose of being a very successful—as Joseph Brambile had thought of her—"lady of the evening" who liked to use her earnings for gambling. She had come to the gambling house to carry out a reconnaissance and, if possible, to find out whether he could pay a visit without having his true identity exposed.

How successfuly Roxanne had played the part was shown when, on her arrival, she was taken into the partners' private office and subjected to questioning about matters that did not pertain to gambling. Jacques had started by wanting to know where she came from, and her reply was that she was visiting Atlanta to decide whether to move there, as she was getting tired of working in Charleston. Asked if she had come to their place in search of clients, showing the contents of her well-filled reticule, she had stated that her only interest was in trying her luck at one or other of their games. They had said they had no objections to this being done, and Hunt warned that they would expect twenty-five percent of any money she was to receive if she should change her mind and take one of the customers to participate in her line of business. Saying the contingency was remote, she had agreed to do as was demanded.

The arrival of Belle and the elderly-looking man had come as something of a shock to the redhead. While she could not imagine why the beautiful Southern girl was dressed and behaving in such an untypical fashion, she had felt sure that it was not for the obvious reason. However, concluding that Belle had not become a prostitute and might not even be pretending to be one, she had decided against going over and satisfying her curiosity by suggesting that they were acquainted on that account. Realizing that the girl must be experiencing the same kind of consternation that she had felt, she had derived a little amusement at seeing the overt glances directed her way and the response when she was caught doing the same.

Hearing the statement made by the girl and seeing the response it was eliciting, Roxanne realized that the playacting had been leading up to it for some reason. While unable to guess what this might be, she decided that she might serve her own and de-Farge's ends by helping out. She had a Henry Derringer pistol loaded, the necessary percussion cap ready for detonation, in her reticule; but it held only a single shot and she had another weapon available that she would be able to use more than once if the need arose, and she felt certain it would. Nevertheless, she refused to let herself be deterred by the danger. In addition to the liking she had formed toward

the girl, who could almost certainly have beaten her using
savate and had willingly engaged in putting on a show instead
of doing so—also insisted upon her keeping all of the gratu-
ties that the enthusiastic audience donated in spite of its deliberately brought about "indecisive" conclusion—she felt sure
de-Farge would not approve if she failed to play a part in
whatever was to come.

*   *   *

Exchanging angry glances, Martin Jacques and David Hunt
started to stalk toward the main faro table. Without needing to
be instructed, a couple of the burly bouncers started to con-
verge on their employers and the rest began to watch the other
players for any sign of taking undue interest in what had been
claimed. Stiffening slightly, knowing what was expected of
him in such circumstances, the dealer for the game of faro
accused of cheating was aware that an examination of the
screw box would probably be demanded by the other players
and anybody with a knowledge of such things would realize
its purpose made the claim valid. Therefore, he prepared to
carry out his instructions by exchanging it for one that was
identical except for being constructed without the embellish-
ments needed for cheating.

"I must ask you to keep control of your wom—!" the
bulkier of the pair began, all trace of amiability having left his
face.

The words came to an end as Jacques and his companion
saw—and were amazed more than puzzled—by what Belle
was doing.

The girl had decided against having a handbag of any kind
with her, and the nature of her attire had prevented her from
bringing even a weapon as small as a Derringer single-shot
pistol or one of its many copies manufactured with ease of
concealability in mind. However, the omission did not mean
she was without adequate means of defending herself. She had,
in fact, come prepared for the contingency that she knew
would arise once her companion was satisfied that cheating
was taking place and she announced this in the way she had
done. Nor was she placing her reliance solely on the bracelet

with the sharpened section of its rim given to her by Captain Anatol de-Farge as a means of defensive or offensive action. She had been warned of the risks that would be entailed, but was counting on the element of surprise giving her an opportunity she intended to make the most of.

Grasping the dainty and fragile-looking parasol at the top of the rolled canopy in her left hand, Belle did not intend to make use of its special function for the moment. Nevertheless, despite realizing that she must carry out her other idea to provide the effect she desired, she found forcing herself with more effort than she had anticipated would be needed when planning for such a contingency. What she intended to do was something that her upbringing came close to revolting against. However, she steeled her resolve by recollecting that she had permitted herself to be stripped to the waist while supposedly fighting with Roxanne Fortescue-Smethers in the ring at Captain Anatol de-Farge's gambling house near Baton Bayou—where there were men who might have recognized her despite the change of hair color and if the mask she wore had been displaced—for a far less important reason than the serious business she was engaged upon this night. Sucking in a quick breath, she compelled herself to use her right hand to give a sharp tug at the waistband of her crinoline dress. Doing so proved this to be a garment in two portions. As was intended and had always happened when she practiced the move before a full-length mirror in the privacy of her room at Rose Greenhow's home, the hem of the skirt opened.

On the girl giving the required quick shaking motion from her hips, the liberated skirt began to slide downward. The unexpected development was followed with interest by the gazes of more than one pair of masculine eyes, but she was concerned only with the effect it was having on the two men. What was brought into view was both satisfying to their lascivious proclivities and puzzling. While the falling away of the garment showed that she was wearing abbreviated white frilly-legged satin pantalets, and that the red slashes of suspender straps descended to support black stockings adding to the allure, she had on sharp-toed black riding boots with moderate heels instead of the kind of footwear that might be ex-

pected to be in accord with the kind of ensemble she had
selected to give credence to her role as "Magnolia Beauregard."

As soon as the girl started the discarding of the skirt, having
been told on the way to the gambling house what would happen—as both had agreed it was practically certain to occur—
when the need to do so arose, Brambile rose and swiftly slid
out the blade of the sword that was concealed in his ebony
walking cane. However, he did not start to put it to use. Instead, he just held it where the clearly razor-sharp and needle-
pointed Toledo steel could be seen. Knowing there could be a
need for an even more potent means of controlling the situation, he sent his right hand to pass with an equal alacrity behind his back beneath the loosely fitting white frock coat, to
emerge holding a Colt 1860 Army Model revolver that had
had its loading lever removed and barrel shortened to two
inches. However, the modification did not cause it to be any
less effective as a weapon at the close quarters he would need
to use it should the situation demand.

"Drop the screw box!" the gambler demanded, leveling
the gun at the dealer. All suggestion of being of advanced
years had fallen away from him, but just a hint of Colonel
Culpepper returned to his voice as he continued dryly, "Or
would you care to take *odds* on avoiding a new head?"

While Brambile was having his command obeyed, at the
other end of the table a potential threat to Belle and himself
was being nullified.

Seeing that one of the massive bouncers was coming her
way, Roxanne stood up with a vehemence that sent her chair
skidding across the well-polished floor and warned him vo-
cally that he should change his mind on the issue. Being employed for bulk and muscle rather than intelligence, he
neglected to accept the suggestion. Thrusting forward his right
arm, he was ready to shove the redhead aside when he found
that his idea was fraught with problems he had not envisaged.
A shake of her right wrist caused a bracelet similar to the one
de-Farge had given to the slender girl to slide down until she
could grasp it by the unsharpened portion.

Knocking the approaching hand aside with her left forearm
and using the skill she had acquired during the real and faked

fights in which she had engaged for the entertainment of de-Farge's customers, the redhead swung the disguised weapon so its cutting edge laid open his cheek. Jerking her elegant dress's skirt with her other hand until it was high enough to allow the required freedom of movement, she used her left foot to give an added impetus as he staggered back, his hands going to the bleeding gash. Tripping, he sat down on the floor with a thud that drove all the breath from his lungs and rendered him incapable of doing anything other than sit there.

"Keep out of it!" Roxanne commanded as men who were acting as dealer and supervisor at a nearby table given over to *chemin de fer* rose from their places.

While speaking, the redhead crouched with the blood-stained bracelet grasped ready for use. The demeanor she presented and the look on her face made her appear to be as dangerous as a bobcat facing up to a pack of hounds. Both being shorter and less heavily built than the bouncer with whom she had dealt so effectively, also being employed for their manipulative skills with a deck of cards rather than the brawn required to deal with recalcitrant players, the pair took the warning she gave to heart and resumed their seats to await developments on the part of others more capable of tackling the furiously glaring woman.

Before either Jacques or Hunt could recover from their surprise and start moving again after the unexpected development had caused them to halt a short distance away, Belle stepped clear of the skirt and went into action. Having disliked the way in which Hunt had looked her over on arrival and since, she made him the first subject of her attention. Gliding forward, she whipped her right leg upward. The way she did so proved she had not forgotten the suggestion made by Captain Alexandre Dartagnan while they were discussing the means she had employed when attempting to go to the assistance of Alfred Higgins on the night of the abortive robbery in Richmond.

Rising between the inadvertently parted thighs of the gambling house's tall and gaunt partner, the toe of Belle's boot—which proved even more efficacious than the footwear worn for savate boxing would have been—struck upon a most vulnerable portion of his anatomy with considerable force. Even as he was letting out a strangled gurgle of agony and folding

over, his assailant gave her attention to his partner, thinking
that the result produced by following Dartagnan's advice made
doing so worthwhile under the prevailing conditions.

However, on this occasion, the girl did not try to use the
same kind of tactics.

Instead, having grasped the parasol just below its handle as
soon as she no longer needed her other hand for helping retain
her balance while delivering the devastating kick, Belle gave
a twist at it in opposite directions with both hands. On separating into two portions, the handle section—which had a
small metal ball on top—was swung in a whiplike upward arc.
Proving to be attached to a coil spring that emerged from being
telescoped into the interior, the ball was given an added impetus as it struck Jacques on the temple with a resounding
thwack. With eyes glazing, his head snapped around and his
bulky body crumpled like a rag doll from which all the stuffing
has suddenly been removed, and he fell flaccidly to the floor.

"Calm yourselves, ladies and gentlemen!" Brambile thundered as the second of the men attacked by the girl went down.
"The charge made by my companion is true. Cheating *is* taking place in this game, and I can prove it!"

Having laid down his sword while speaking, the gambler
quickly removed a silver whistle from his left-side outer jacket
pocket. In answer to the shrill and loud blast he gave upon it,
the front and other doors of the room were burst open. Soldiers, men wearing the distinctive blue uniforms of the Atlanta
Police Department, and a few civilians entered swiftly. The
latter group included Alfred Higgins, whose skill at manipulating his "twirls" had gained them admittance, and their surprise arrival had allowed them to silence any chance of an
outcry being given by the staff who were working other than
in the main room. Since they were all carrying revolvers, their
entrance caused the remainder of the gambling house's staff
to put aside any thoughts of hostilities.

Nor did any of the people who had been playing the various
games raise any objections over what had happened. There
were no laws prohibiting gambling in the city any more than
elsewhere through the South, so they were all motivated by a
desire to find out whether the allegations of cheating could be

substantiated. Introducing himself and finding that he was known by reputation if not sight to a number of the crowd, Brambile soon satisfied them on the matter by demonstrating the use of the screw box and describing how other malpractices had been carried out. Having been told that they would be able to recoup whatever losses they had incurred that evening—although some of the more senior officers wanted to know what had caused the gambler and "Miss Beauregard" to arrive so fortuitously and accepted the promise made by Colonel Charles Jeremiah Mason that he would submit a report in writing the following day—they all settled down to await the return of the money.

While the men were attending to things, Belle went to thank Roxanne for not having exposed her as well as for preventing the participation of the bouncer and other members of the staff. In return, the redhead assured Belle that the feeling regarding not having been given away were mutual and that things were far from being as they appeared in her case, then promised to make a full explanation at a more propitious moment. Belle agreed to the arrangement and suggested that Roxanne should avail herself of the offer to recoup her losses, and she said that she would be delighted to do so with perhaps a little added to the actual sum. She also remarked with a twinkle in her eyes that it was a pity Jacques and Hunt did not have a ring set up so they could earn themselves some money by entertaining the gamblers with another stirring and profitable "fight." Also amused by the proposition, the girl said she doubted whether her superior would be in favor of her taking part in such a thing.

* * *

"I would like to congratulate you on a most excellent piece of work last night, Miss Boyd, Mr. Brambile," Colonel Charles Mason announced once the pair were seated across from him at his desk. They had been asked to be there at nine o'clock in the morning and had felt it incumbent upon them to arrive punctually, which he showed signs of appreciating. "When he recovered from your—attack, ma'am, Hunt proved to be *most* cooperative in the hope of saving his neck. With Jacques being dead and unable to deny the charge, he claimed he was not involved in the blackmailing which obtained military secrets for the North and had, in fact, only learned such was taking place that evening. We found all we needed to know and retrieved all the latest acquisitions from the safe which he opened for us. There will be nothing more going to the Yankees.''

''Do the names of the victims have to be made public, sir?'' the girl asked, having learned after leaving together what brought Roxanne Fortescue-Smethers to the gambling house so fortuitously and hoping to avoid having the cause of Lieutenant Phillipe de-Farge's suicide become known.

''We don't intend to do so,'' Mason declared. ''It won't achieve anything other than ruin some promising careers, and I feel sure *none* of them will ever make a similar mistake after I or the commanding general have interviewed them. I trust you don't feel too badly over what happened to Jacques, Miss Boyd?''

''I don't,'' Belle replied. ''Although I would have preferred that it didn't happen.''

Having been told before she left the gambling house that the blow to the temple from her spring-loaded weapon had caused such a severe concussion that its recipient died without regaining consciousness, the girl had felt only a slight remorse. The man she had struck down was an enemy of the South—who could also be considered a traitor, it having been discovered from Hunt that he was born in Nashville, Tennessee, a state that had espoused the Confederate cause—working for financial gain rather than patriotism or support of the Union.

Belle had taken additional solace from also having been convinced that, having the accusation of cheating made, the pair would not have hesitated to take reprisals of a severe nature against herself and Brambile. Considering the lecherous way in which Jacques and Hunt had looked at her, probably these would have even entailed rape where she was concerned. What was more, she had accepted when becoming a member of the Confederate States Secret Service that her duties might entail the taking of another human being's life. It was also her sworn intention to kill George Tollinger and Alfred Barmain if she was granted an opportunity.

By her action when dealing with Jacques, Belle Boyd had taken another step along the road that would lead to her becoming known as the Rebel Spy.

PART THREE

MISSION INTO ENEMY TERRITORY

CHAPTER ONE

You Sound Like Johnny Rebs!

"Howdy, fellers," Captain Jethro "Stone" Hart greeted with his Texas drawl made rougher and more crude-sounding than was usually the case, as he and Sergeant Standish "Waggles" Harrison rode into view along a small track leading from a clump of trees to where a corporal and two cavalrymen in Union blue were approaching from the opposite direction. "You headed for Washington?"

"Sure," the corporal answered, looking in disdain at the pair and something close to envy when starting to study the excellent quality of the horse each rode while leading another just as good. However, neither he nor the enlisted men were showing any surprise at seeing from where they had emerged. "We're on furlough. How about you?"

"Taking these hosses to our colonel in Glissade," Stone lied, noticing that the shorter and older of the two enlisted men was eyeing him in a more speculative fashion than the non-com. "Trust *him* to have fine critters like these here, you should see what *we* get give' to ride."

"That's for sure!" Waggles declared vehemently, making no attempt to hide the fact that his origins also were in Texas, although having no need to give the words a simulated suggestion of possessing lower educational standards than was the case with his superior. As he was speaking, the gaze of the older cavalryman swung his way and became more contemplative. "Hell, I wouldn't've been seed *dead* riding what I've been give' was I back to home."

If the Captain and Sergeant had been dressed in the usual fashion as required by their having been seconded to the staff of General John Bell Hood's Texas Brigade of the Confederate States Army, the speculation would have been understandable. However, instead of their smart and well-cared-for cadet-gray cavalry attire, they had on slovenly uniforms of a style similar

to that of the three Yankees seen by Waggles just in time for
them to halt and allow the third member of the party to take
cover with the packhorse that was carrying all they needed for
the journey they were making. Realizing that the trio were
coming their way, Stone and his noncom advanced to see what
could be done to avoid letting the presence of their companion
become discovered.

Just over six feet tall and in his midtwenties, there was none
of Stone's usual smartness of appearance about him. His black
hair showed untidily from beneath a grubby U.S. Cavalry kepi
and covered the cheeks of his handsome face with stubble.
Selected to conceal the fact as far as was possible, as was his
deliberately slouching posture, his slender frame gave no suggestion of its whipcord power. Of a bad fit, despite the triple
chevrons of a sergeant attached out of alignment on his
sleeves, the rest of his uniform was no more clean and gave
suggestions of neglect rather than hard usage. If looked at
more closely than was happening, it would have been obvious
that the saber in the slings at the left side of his waistbelt was
of more excellent manufacture and kept in better condition
than his attire implied should be the case. The closed top of
the holster on the right prevented the turned-forward walnut
butt of his Colt Model of 1860 Army revolver from being seen.
If it had been examined, its first-rate condition would have
indicated that it, too, was better maintained than his slovenly
demeanor would have led one to expect.

Matching his superior in height, around ten years older,
Waggles was more heavily built without being bulky. His
rusty-brown hair just as uncombed and his leathery brown un-
emotional face also in need of a shave, he had taken care to
ensure that he was no more smartly dressed. Nevertheless, the
weapons that duplicated those of Stone—except for the saber
being of a slightly lower quality—were equally indicative of
regular care and attention.

Standing in concealment but able to watch what was taking
place, Belle Boyd was ready to prevent any sound leaving
either of her two excellent riding horses or the pack animal
left in her keeping. Her face streaked by dirt and hair covered
with a black Burnside hat liberally coated with trail dust, she
had on clothes similar to those worn by the two Texans. How-

ever, the weapon at the left-side slings of her belt was an *épée de combat* made to her specifications by a master cutler in Richmond who had at first seemed puzzled by her insistence upon the features she required—such as a knuckle bow hand guard on the handle—and then, accepting that she knew exactly what she wanted, produced a superlative example of his workmanship. It was designed to be easily taken apart, and, when necessary, the blade would be transported in a hollow walking stick while the handle would be concealed among feminine attire in her baggage. Chosen to ride properly in her Union Cavalry–pattern holster was a Colt Model of 1851 Navy Belt Pistol, a six-shot .36-caliber revolver despite its name, with a seven-and-a-half-inch octagonal barrel.

How the girl came to be in enemy territory a few miles east of Washington was the result of her latest assignment for the Confederate States Secret Service.

On the night before the contingent from the Richmond section of the Confederate States Secret Service returned to their base, Colonel Charles Jeremiah Mason had entertained them, Roxanne Fortescue-Smethurst, and Captain Anatol de-Farge at dinner. He had thanked everybody concerned for the excellent results obtained because of their efforts. With that done, he had stated—albeit, the Southron girl suspected, more tongue-in-cheek than would have been the case when they first met—that he still did not think such duties should be handled by ladies, making it clear that he included the redhead in the category, even though on this occasion they had proved to be of the greatest assistance. He had even gone so far as to state that the successful outcome could not have been achieved without them.

With the formalities over, Ole Dixie had proved to be an excellent host and far from as hidebound as he had first given Belle the impression of being. In fact, she had thoroughly enjoyed herself and been amused by the way he had clearly relished the amusing anecdotes that Alfred Higgins provided. While she and Roxanne had been freshening up in the room provided for that purpose, they had derived amusement from agreeing that it was a pity they could not put on the kind of entertainment they had provided for the clientele of de-Farge's gambling house. On a more serious level, before they parted company at the end of the evening, the girl had been told by the gambler that he had arranged with their host that he and the redhead would give their services as agents as and when required. This was to prove most useful when the forces of the Union gained control of the Mississippi River beyond where it flowed through Baton Bayou Parish.

There had been one outcome of the affair that was to prove beneficial for Belle in the future, although she did not learn of Mason's involvement until long after. Using his connections with General Robert E. Lee and other prominent Southrons, he had caused her to be given the rank and pay of a captain in the Confederate States Army as a means of helping her obtain cooperation from officers in the line of her duties. There had been no objections to the arrangement from Rose Greenhow, who had attained the status of full colonel for the same reason and had already made a proposal that her niece should be granted the rank given to all the male members of their organization.

Unaware of the way in which her career was to be given the assistance of an official military rank, also an addition to her earnings that was most acceptable, Belle had not been allowed to rest on her laurels when she rejoined her aunt. Nor could she complain that she was not put to a useful purpose in giving service to the Southern cause. During the next six months, she had carried out three missions to deliver and collect information from agents that took her into Union-held territory. All had entailed traveling in disguise and, on two, her skill at riding astride had brought her to safety in spite of her being hotly pursued by Yankee cavalrymen. When she was not required for such work, she had occupied her time by carrying out training in subjects that would be of use in future assignments.

In between her missions, the girl was constantly improving her fighting skills without using weapons. Nor was her ability to handle a sword—especially the new *épée de combat* when it arrived, so as to ensure that she became fully conversant with its weight, balance, and special peculiarities—and other weapons, even those of unconventional and, until put into effect, unsuspected devices employed to defeat Martin Jacques and David Hunt neglected. In fact, she soon could use each with even more efficiency and was satisfied she could do so even to the extent of killing should the need arise. More of her time had been spent being instructed in techniques of lockpicking and housebreaking by Higgins. She also developed her use of disguises to an even higher degree than she had when employing her flair for such things while trying to find members of the Secret Service.

There had been one disappointment for Belle as the weeks went by. Rose had had a request passed for all Southern agents to keep watch for and seek news of the whereabouts of George Tollinger and Alfred Barmain. While there had been occasional reports to confirm that they were now serving with a "liberal" section of the Union's Secret Service, which generally operated in opposition to those members led by the much more efficient Allan Pinkerton, neither had ever been anywhere near the places where Belle had carried out her assignments. However, this had in no way lessened her determination to be avenged upon them for the murder of her parents and destruction of Baton Royale Manor.

The arrival of the message that brought the girl to her present position had been considered of such vital urgency that taking action could not be delayed. Knowing Doctor Fritz Conried would not have taken the chances involved in sending the news and request for assistance by carrier pigeon unless regarding the state of affairs he of necessity could only briefly describe as being of the utmost gravity, Rose was informed by her superiors in Richmond that action must be taken as soon as possible to discover how great a threat to the Confederate cause was being posed and, if necessary, nullify it. The problem with which she was faced had been that only Belle of all her agents was immediately available.

Despite having faith in the proven ability of her niece, Rose had had qualms over sending her upon the assignment. Its nature was far different from anything she had done previously. However, against that, she had already made an of necessity brief contact with Conried on her second mission when collecting information he had gathered and knew the terrain through which she would have to pass. With this and the other factors in mind, putting aside thoughts of the dangers that would be involved, the beautiful Southron woman had con-

ferred with Belle and decided how the duty could be performed. They had agreed from the start that it could not be
carried out without assistance, which had raised the point of
what form this would take. None of her fellow operatives
could be recalled from their respective tasks in time to be of
use. Unfortunately, neither she—because time had not permitted them to discuss such matters even if either had been inclined to do so instead of adhering to the wise policy of what
a later generation would term the need to know—nor Rose
was aware of how big an organization Conried controlled except that they assumed its members would not be numerous
and were unlikely to possess the kind of skills that might be
needed.

As the result of the deliberations, it had been decided that
Belle would be given the escort of the two members of General
Hood's Texas Brigade who were available and possessed the
requisite qualities. Chief among these had been a willingness
to accept the risks of being captured wearing uniforms and
posing as Union soldiers, thereby rendering them almost certain to be shot as spies if they should be captured. Taking
advantage of her skill in equestrian matters, which her escort
also possessed to an equally high standard, they were to travel
on horseback and ride relay on two mounts apiece as a means
of covering the distance in the quickest possible time. Excellent in quality though their mounts were, the speed at which
they could travel would be limited somewhat by having along
a pack animal carrying all they required. While it was their
intention to do everything possible to avoid coming into contact with anybody even before reaching Union territory, to
avoid arousing interest that might be heard of and reported by
Yankee spies, they had been given the means of offering an
explanation for their presence should they fail to do so.

If granted the opportunity, which the abilities as a scout
possessed by one of her escort made it likely could occur, the
girl was to assume the clothing suitable for her pose and carry
documents to suggest that she was a maid delivering the property of the wife of a Union general. For the remainder of the
time after leaving Confederate terrain, she would travel in the
same kind of close-to-regulation uniform as her companions,
which had been copied from the kind issued—to some of the

numerous regiments of volunteers formed with patriotic fervor or for political motives in the North. Because these allowed considerable variation in the kind of weapons provided, this allowed her to carry the *épeé de combat*, which had been made to her specifications by a master cutler in Richmond on the slings at the left side of her officially designed waistbelt, and a Colt Model of 1853 Navy revolver butt-forward in the regulation-patterned holster on the right.

To support the identities they intended to give themselves if unable to avoid meeting with Union troops, the trio had been provided with the necessary documents to establish the supposed veracity of the claim. As they all had accents indicative of origins being other than Northern, these alleged that they were Southerners who espoused the Union's cause out of an opposition to slavery. Producing these special items had created no problems for Belle's section of the Secret Service. Enough officers of all ranks had transferred allegiance to the Army of the Confederate States when it became obvious that war could not be avoided—Stone Hart having been one—for the South to follow the general organization of their Northern adversaries. Therefore, it had been known roughly what form the genuine items were likely to take. Furthermore, especially with the pose being that of men serving in a recently formed volunteer regiment—few of which were led by officers having been more than a minimal length in such positions of command—any discrepancies in the paperwork could be explained away as being due to inexperience with the way things were done in the Union Army. Having looked the documents over, Waggles had said dryly that they were more likely to be accepted by members of regular outfits if they did not quite conform to regulations, as such was only to be expected of hurriedly recruited and less-than-thoroughly-trained crowds of "weekend soldiers" led by "ninety-day wonders."

Because of the care that was taken in selecting the route they traveled, Belle and her escort had made good time and remained unseen until they were on the last few miles from their destination. From the beginning, she had taken a liking to the two Texans. In return, they had very quickly gained respect for her having sufficient ability as a horsewoman to ensure that she did not slow them down. Although she had not

been able to show how well she could shoot, as doing so might
be heard and investigated, their admiration had grown after
having seen a demonstration of her skill at wielding the *épée
de combat* on the first night after they had made camp. Stone
had said that he and his sergeant had been told of her abilities
and achievements when asked to volunteer for the escort duty,
but admitted they had felt some misgivings over a young
woman being in command of such a potentially dangerous
assignment. However, both of them had stated they now believed there was no need for concern on that account.

On hearing from Waggles that there were the three Yankee
cavalrymen approaching and were so near, Belle and Stone
had decided against taking cover. It was felt advisable that she
should rely upon her disguise and let herself be seen at such
close quarters, but if the subterfuge was detected, it might not
be possible to silence all three without shooting, and there was
no way of knowing how many other members of the Union
Army or even civilians who were almost certain to have
Northern sympathies were within hearing distance to be at-
tracted by it. Therefore, she had proposed another means of
coping with the situation. Agreeing that it stood a good chance
of working and having the means to do so, the preparations
had been carried out swiftly. Then the Texans had ridden into
view and, at least until the conversation was commenced, there
was nothing to indicate that they were suspected of being other
than they appeared.

That desirable state of affairs was brought to an end.

"Hey!" the shorter of the enlisted men yelled, making a
grab at the closed flap of his holster. "You sound like Johnny
Rebs!"

"Hold hard there, soldier!" Stone thundered, without offering to duplicate the action of the Yankee soldier where arm-
ing himself was concerned. "God damn it, I'm getting sick of
being told *that*. We hail from *North* Texas, so why the hell
wouldn't we sound like Johnny Rebs?"

"Show him them fancy papers we've been give', Sto—
Serge!" Waggles suggested with a similar appearance of
wrath. "Happen he can't read, I reckon the corp' there does
'n' can tell him what they say."

"What papers're those?" the corporal asked, showing suspicion without making a move toward the holster on his weapon belt.

"Here," Stone growled, drawing the appropriate document from the inside jacket of his tunic and holding it forward while wondering how its contents would be received.

Accepting the sheet of paper and opening it out, silently mouthing some of the longer words, the corporal began to read what was printed on it. It stated that Jethro Hart of Clarksville, Red River County, North Texas, had sworn allegiance to the Union and enrolled in the Third New Mexico Hussars. Although he had never heard of such a regiment, he saw nothing in the other's appearance to make him doubt its existence.

Being a long-serving member of the regular Army, the corporal had little other than contempt for volunteer outfits, and the one named looked as if it was just about the same as all the rest. However, he was aware that most of their noncoms were very rank conscious, and he was too wise to express or even let his true feelings become obvious. The three-bar looked as though he could be a mean son of a bitch if riled, and the enlisted man would probably prove no easy mark should there be trouble. What was more, seeing as the corporal and his companions were headed to Washington for a furlough, the last thing he wanted was for anything to delay their getting there. With that in mind, he folded the paper.

"That's what she says, Serge," the noncom declared, handing back the document. "No offense tooken, I hope."

"Nary an offense," Stone asserted, and having replaced the paper, reached back to take a bottle filled with brown liquid from the pouch of his McClellan saddle. As was the case with much of their equipment, the South had obtained enough of these now-becoming-standard-issue U.S. Army rigs for there being nothing untoward in he and his companion using one apiece. Drawing the cork, he held it forward. "Here, to show it, you boys all take yourselves a good pull of this sippin' whiskey. It's good stuff, snuck from Major Backstead. He pays for it with money saved from buying those goddamned plugs we gets for hosses."

Watching what happened, Waggles reached in what ap-

peared to be a casual gesture until able to thumb open the flap
of his holster. If the offer was not accepted, another means
would have to be found to deal with the contingency. It was
very soon apparent that the need would not arise. Taking the
bottle, the corporal did as was requested. After having taken
a long and appreciative pull at the contents, he passed it to the
taller enlisted man. Showing no greater reluctance, the recipient drank just as deeply. Then, as if wanting to make up for
the suspicions he had aroused about the Texans, the last of the
trio duplicated the actions of his companions.

Also keeping the men under observation, Belle soon decided that de-Farge had not been exaggerating when speaking
of how quickly the powerful opiate took effect. Before the last
of the three had handed the bottle back to Stone, the corporal
swayed and slid limply sideways from his horse. The taller of
the enlisted men following him down a moment later and the
shorter joined them on the ground. Once there, they lay
breathing heavily without any other movement than the steady
rise and fall of their chests. Grinning broadly, Waggles prevented their horses from moving away on being so suddenly
deprived of riders.

"I never yet saw a Yankee who could take his liquor,"
Stone declared in his normal voice as his sergeant completed
the task and he waved for the girl to come out of her place of
concealment. When she arrived, he went on, "That stuff sure
worked like you said it would. Not that I even for a moment
thought it wouldn't."

"Or me," Belle stated cheerfully. "I hoped there would be
a chance for me to try it out on somebody, though. I didn't
have the heart to do it on any of my friends."

"Well, I'd say you've for sure got 'round to doing it, and
that stuff certainly works fast," the captain drawled. "How
long will they be under?"

"A couple of hours at least, Anatol de-Farge claimed, with
the amount I used," the girl replied. "And he's been right for
the rest of what he told me. They didn't show any sign of
having been able to taste it, and the last one went down before
he could even realize, much less take warning from, what what
was happening to the other two."

"Then we'll get them and their horses in a clearing back there to sleep it out like we planned," Stone said. "I'm willing to bet that when they wake up and find their horses hobbled there and all their money still on them, they'll head for Washington and their furlough instead of coming to Glissade to look for us."

CHAPTER TWO

I'm *Absolutely,* Positively *Certain*— I Think!

"Well, it seems that you called the play right, Stone," Belle Boyd remarked with satisfaction. "Those three will have recovered long before this and Waggles hasn't seen them coming back to the regiment to tell what happened to them."

With the unconscious Yankee soldiers disposed of as was planned, the trio had continued their interrupted journey. They had covered the remaining distance until arriving at their present location without seeing any further signs of human beings. Once among an area of woodland about half a mile away from the small town of Glissade that the girl remembered from her previous visit, they had halted to await sundown. The last time she had gone to see Doctor Fritz Conried, she had ridden up through the darkness dressed in masculine civilian attire. However, although there had been no problems caused by her doing so, he had said he would prefer for any further visits she paid to be made in a less noticeable fashion. Accepting that he knew what was best for his own and her safety, she had kept the suggestion in mind when making preparations for calling again.

The girl had just rejoined Captain Stone Hart and Sergeant Waggles Harrison where they were waiting with the horses in a clearing. While she was absent, she had donned the items of feminine attire chosen for making contact with, which had brought in one of the panniers carried by the packhorse. With her recollection of the precaution requested during the previous visit and the need to limit the weight carried by the animal, she had accepted the need to restrict the clothing to what she felt would be best suited for her purposes. Over a different kind of masculine garments, which served to show off her slenderly curvaceous, all-too-obviously female bodily contours far more than those worn during the journey through Union territory, she had on a black blouse and matching skirt that gave the appearance of being a single dress of the kind generally supplied as working attire for one kind of domestic servant. To add to the suggestion of such employment, her black hair—which she kept cut short to allow the wearing of one of the wigs she used even when in the safety of Richmond society to prevent its condition arousing speculation—was concealed beneath a white cotton mobcap that was in keeping with the rest of her outer costume.

There was, Belle had explained to the Texans, a good reason for her to adopt such garb that would also have been used if the need arose during the journey through Union territory on the way to Glissade. It was intended to give the appearance of being a maid while walking through the town just after night had fallen. The regiment of regular Union Cavalry to which the three soldiers they had left drugged belonged were camped on the outskirts at the west side and another to the north of the town. Based upon his own experiences as an officer in the Union Army prior to returning to serve the South, Stone had agreed with her observation that the wives of particularly the senior officers would have such servants and, unlike in the South, few would be Negresses. Therefore, her arrival in such a guise would arouse less curiosity and speculation over a stranger walking through the streets, since the local population were likely to assume she was just a maid from the camp carrying out a task for her mistress.

When making the explanation, the girl had not said whom she was going to meet in Glissade. Nor, as the Texans had realized why this was, had either of them asked about it. Instead, the arrangement was for them to remain where they were until she returned. Or, should they hear the kind of disturbance that would indicate she had either been captured or killed, they were to assume the same applied to the man she visited and go straight back to Richmond with the news. The same would apply if she failed to rejoin them by sunrise, since this would mean that she had been taken by the Yankees in some way that prevented her from making any noise to warn them of what had happened. There must *not*, she insisted, emphasizing the word of denial, be any attempt to find out her fate, much less a rescue should she have been taken alive. Regardless of how they might feel, she must be regarded as expendable. That was, she had said without any suggestion of

being dramatic, one of the penalties to be accepted serving as
a spy.

"I reckon I just about ought to know how soldiers think
by now," Stone replied to the comment about the behavior of
the three Union cavalrymen when recovering from the effects
of the drugged drink. Then a note of concern came into his
voice: "But will you be safe going into town dressed like
that?"

"Of course I will," Belle declared, and went on with the
kind of humor her companions often employed and, she felt,
would enjoy now. "I'm *absolutely*, positively *certain*—I
think."

For all the levity, Belle was taking precautions for her protection should some emergency arise. Aware that there was no
way she could have either her Colt or particularly the *épée de
combat* with her—the unconventional design of the latter being
certain to arouse curiosity if seen even in poor lighting conditions—she was going to leave them with the Texans. Instead,
having put on her outer garments, she had donned her razor-
edged bracelet. In addition, its canopy having been replaced
by one of cheap black material such as might be expected in
the possession of the kind of person she was pretending to be,
she would also be carrying the parasol with the telescopic coil-
spring-powered billy as a further means of defense.

As was the case with all of the girl's other feminine clothing, none of which she had with her, the skirt of her attire was
modified to allow easy removal. However, instead of the brief
pantalets and black stockings that had diverted Jaques and
Hunt to her advantage in Atlanta, she had a man's figure-
hugging open-necked thin black shirt and equally snugly con-
forming matching riding breeches underneath. These were to
serve as the kind of distraction provided by the sensual un-
dergarment worn at the gambling house should the need arise.
Because they, too, would be concealed by the skirt, she was
wearing the black riding boots, which she felt confident would
once again prove most efficacious if an attack *á la savate* was
called for.

Wanting to avoid any such means of self-defense if possible, regardless of how effective she knew them to be, Belle
was carrying a bulky and cheap-looking black reticule in

which, among some of the feminine items a person of the kind
she was pretending to be could carry without arousing suspicions in the event of a search, was the bottle containing the
remaining whiskey laced with the kind of opiate intended for
use with the ring she was given by Captain Anatol de-Farge.
She was satisfied that there was still enough of the potent
liquor to serve her purposes. If anybody should stop and question her, it was her intention to reply with the pronounced
French accent she had learned to employ so adequately that it
made the Southern inflection in her normal voice indistinguish-
able. The drugged drink was to be used only as a last resort.

None of the precautions had proved necessary.

For all the calm way in which she had spoken to the Texans, the girl was experiencing a little tension while walking
briskly and with apparent nonchalance through the streets of
the town. She knew that, with the exception of the man she
had come to meet, everybody she encountered was a potential
enemy. However, as she had anticipated and gambled upon
being the case—except for a couple of soldiers who took her
for what she was pretending to be and made an improper suggestion without attempting to follow it up and needing to be
answered in some suitable fashion—the few people whom she
passed on the not brightly lit streets paid no attention to her.

Arriving at the combination residence and surgery of Doctor Conried, she found the latter to be in darkness, although
lights showed from the former. Much to her relief, it was he
who came in response to her knock on the front door. He was
as she remembered him, even to the casual way in which he
was dressed. Tall, burly, and gray-haired, he had a cheerful
Germanic cast of features, although his New England mode of
speech had not the slightest trace of an accent suggestive of
his being of that race. She had no idea why a man from that
Northern region where the majority of the population were so
firm in their support for the Union had elected to become a
spy for the South, being content with knowing he was considered by Rose Greenhow as being one of the best and most
reliable of all who worked from inside Yankee territory. Aware
of how urgent the matter must be, instead of thinking about
the subject of his motivation, she commenced the ritual she
knew would be expected of her and serve as a means of iden-

tification in case she was not remembered from her previous visit. As she had worn masculine attire on that occasion, she felt it possible that this might indeed happen until he was granted a closer look at her face.

"Southrons, hear your country call you!" Belle announced sotto voce after having gazed about her surreptitiously yet thoroughly to be sure nobody else was close enough to hear the first line of the vigorously patriotic verses written by General Albert Pike of the Confederate States Army to replace the far more bland words that Daniel D. Emmett had penned for his minstrel song "Dixie."

"Up lest death or worse befall you!" Conried replied correctly with the second line and no louder, indicating that he was alone in the house and they could conduct the meeting for which the girl had been sent in response to the message he had dispatched by carrier pigeon in privacy and safety. "Come in, please!"

Despite the importance of the information and the need for urgency in having a response to it stressed by the doctor, if he was surprised or disappointed by finding a woman had been sent to meet him, he showed no indication of it. Rather, he accepted without comment the girl's explanation that she and her companions had considered her to be the one best suited for avoiding attracting attention on the way through the town to pay the visit.

Taking Belle into the surgery, explaining as he had the time before that doing so would be expected if anybody should have seen her arrival, he drew the curtains after turning up the lamp he had carried to the front door. Again, he said, this would not arouse speculation, since he would not carry out any examination of a female patient without making sure that whatever undressing might be required could not be seen from outside. Asking her to strip to the waist, to give support to the pretense of her being there for medical reasons should anybody such as his currently absent housekeeper come in unexpectedly—precaution she heartily approved of and had no qualms of carrying out under the prevailing conditions—he waited until this was done and the masculine shirt was concealed beneath the well-worn black leather couch, upon which she had seated herself in accordance with his instructions. Then, having changed into the white coat he wore when engaged in his professional duties and hung his stethoscope around his neck, he wasted no time in getting down to business.

Before Belle had heard many words, she decided that there was justification for the summons. What was more, the situation described by Conried was going to need being given urgent attention by herself and her two companions from Texas. She also realized that what the doctor had discovered and was disclosing could have the potential for turning the course of the war in the favor of the Union. At the very least, if the device he described so graphically was as effective as he claimed it to be, it was going to cause the South enormous loss of lives.

On hearing the name of the inventor of the device, the girl had realized she knew something about him. A couple of years earlier, Christopher Burke had made a tour of Southern plantations trying to interest the owners in a machine to perform the picking of cotton, obviating the need for numerous human hands to perform the task. While it might have made such a thing possible, it had proved to be complex and costly to operate, as well as liable to breakdown and the necessity to purchase expensive spare parts. As if these faults were not sufficient, the device was prone to explode with sudden violence and spread flames over a fair distance around it. Therefore, he and it had become a laughingstock even in regions where it had not been demonstrated. The last thing she had heard about Burke was that he had returned north expressing a bitter hatred of all Southrons because they declined to buy and use his machines, even though he had repeatedly promised all the faults would be corrected prior to delivery.

The thing she had to do, the girl told herself, was see the weapon described by the doctor, if possible, and then decide upon what action must be taken.

*   *   *

Even at a distance of close to a quarter of a mile, which was as close as Belle Boyd and Captain Stone Hart could approach where they were originating from, the continuous roar of detonations was awesome to the ears and the device that was producing them made a sight that was frightening in its potential. It went far beyond anything in her comprehension, and he had never heard or seen a single weapon capable of creating the effect. In fact, he felt sure even a number of trained riflemen at company strength could not have been able to produce such a rate of fire by shooting one after another in their most rapid succession.

Good fortune had continued to favor Belle in her mission. Doctor Fritz Conried had informed her that the weapon that had caused him so much concern was to be demonstrated to some senior officers the following afternoon. His assertion that it would be possible for an unsuspected observation to be carried out from some nearby woodland had proved correct. Having arrived there without being detected, she and Stone had left Sergeant Waggles Harrison to keep the horses quiet and under control while they moved into a point of vantage on foot. They had watched the spectators assembling where a small man in civilian clothes, whom she recognized as being Christopher Burke on being handed field glasses by Stone, was seated behind and showing the potential of the revolutionary weapon he had invented. A larger civilian was kneeling at the right of it and clearly acting as an assistant for its operation.

"Land's sakes!" the girl exclaimed, lowering the field glasses. In her concern, she inadvertently gave a clue to the identity of her informant. "The doctor was *right*. That damned thing *could* change the whole course of the War if the Yankees get enough of them. I've never even imagined there could be anything like it. Why, it fires much faster than is being claimed for the Williams gun of our's that I've heard talk about around Richmond."[1]

"I've not run across one of them yet either," Stone admitted, "but I've heard they're pretty fair and can throw out around sixty-five one-pounder shells a minute. Which's better than those twenty-five-shot Bilinghurst Requa Batteries the Yankees use can turn loose. There was talk before I came south about something called the Agar Coffee Mill gun being on its way, but none had come into service when I left. Do you reckon that thing is one of them?"[2]

[1] *Information regarding the Williams rapid-fire gun is given in* THE REBEL SPY.
[2] *The use to which one Agar Coffee Mill gun was to be put is told in* THE DEVIL GUN.

"Not if what I heard about Christopher Burke is correct," Belle denied. "I'd say he's far too much the egotist to let somebody else's name be used for *his* invention. Do you think that thing is as dangerous as I do, Stone?"

"If it's *not* . . ." the Texan replied in a grim tone. He was thinking of the main disadvantage that applied to the Requa and even more so to the eighty-five to four hundred and fifty barreled Vandenburg Volley Gun already in service with the Union Army as he continued, ". . . it'll surely do until something that *is* dangerous comes along. Like I said, its fires faster than anything I've ever seen or heard tell of, and it will be much easier to move around fast when needed."[3]

The device that was causing so much concern for Belle and Stone was mounted on a small metal tripod instead of the modified artillery carriage that was necessary for the other rapid-fire weapons to become available during the War Between the States. At the rear end of the barrel what was obviously the mechanism was housed in something shaped like an oblong box. Through one side of this, the metallic cartridges in snugly fitting loops on a canvas belt entered a slot to be extracted one after another by some means and fed into the chamber. With the powder discharged and the bullet expelled, the spent case was ejected through a hole in the top of the box and the now-empty belt came out at the side opposite where it entered.

On the belt in use reaching its end, while Burke was drawing it free, the man assisting him placed one that was fully loaded into the slot in the weapon at the other side. When this had been drawn onward a short distance by the inventor, be resumed firing. However, having shown how swiftly the process could be carried out, he sent off only a few more rounds before stopping once again. Then he came to his feet and walked toward the observers.

Such was the apparent simplicity of the operation and the speed by which reloading could be carried out, that the rate of fire attained was far greater than any contemporary multiple-shot mechanism could produce.

---

[3] *How Belle Boyd was later brought into contact with a Vandenburg Volley Gun is told in* THE COLT AND THE SABRE.

"It's *that* deadly, in your opinion?" Belle queried, wanting to satisfy herself there was adequate reason for the drastic line of action she was contemplating.

"They'd come as one hell of a shock to the troops they were first used against. Likely cause a rout and fast withdrawal, too. There's only one thing, though."

"What is it?"

"The speed that gun fires, the barrel and machinery must get hot enough to give plenty of trouble," the Texan estimated, unwittingly suggesting a serious problem that Burke had discovered and was taking steps to prevent letting become apparent to the delegation who had come from Washington to witness the demonstration. "Unless he's come up with some way to cope with it, I'd reckon that its works would soon jam so tight it couldn't go on throwing lead."

"Then we *can't* let the Yankees put them into production," the girl asserted.

"There's a chance they won't do that, going by what I've come to know about the way the top brass thinks. It always looked to me that they just about always shy away from every kind of improvement that's offered no matter how good you might reckon it would be for the men who'll have to do the fighting. Every time a repeating rifle even was offered while I was with the Yankee Army, they started saying how it's too complicated to use and, anyway, issuing them would cause the troops to spray lead around promiscuously instead of aiming carefully. The same's already been said by our high muckety-mucks about the Agar."

"Then why have these high muckety-mucks, as you uncouth Texans say, come to see it?"

"Could be because he's got some influential backing at the capital and the top brass figure they've got to make a show. I don't know whether you noticed, but there isn't even a brigadier general down there. Fact being, there's only one full colonel even, and from the look of him, he's a quartermaster not serving in the field. The rest are the same. I reckon they've been sent along and will go back to give a report for higher up about what they've seen."

"And then what will happen?"

"Unless things have changed a heap up here, which I

wouldn't count on a whole heap, seeing the same kind of thinking's going on down in the South, there'll be some considerable talk about what to do next before anything is decided.''

"And nothing might happen?" Belle inquired, knowing a man's life could be at stake as a result of what the answer should be.

"That'll depend on how much influence is behind him," the Texan judged, noticing the intensity with which the girl was speaking. "Likely they'll have the gun sent down for testing and then decide whether or not to put it into production.''

"But dare we take the chance on that damnable thing not being accepted for some reason?" the girl wanted to know.

"How are we going to stop it happening?" Stone inquired.

"Any way we can," Belle replied, and her manner became redolent of resolve that was chilling in its intensity when coming from one so beautiful and feminine in every aspect, except for her attire once again being that of a Union soldier in which she had traveled to Glissade. "And I don't rule out killing Burke so he can't have any more of them made."

CHAPTER THREE

You've Saved *Me* from Having to Kill Him!

Christopher Burke was in a far from amiable mood as he sat in the dining room of the small house just beyond the fringes of Glissade that he had selected as being suitable for his needs. The house was within a reasonable distance of the contacts he had established in Washington, yet far enough away to avoid too close supervision of his efforts and sufficiently secluded to let him carry out his work in privacy. He had felt the latter point to be a necessity when he embarked upon the project that he felt would bring the acclaim he desired and offer the means to take revenge upon a certain section of the population against whom he had what a later generation would describe as being a close to paranoiac hatred.

No more than five feet four in height, with mouse-brown hair allowed to grow long in the hope of hiding the way it was thinning on top of his dome-shaped skull from being noticeable, Burke had pale and acne-scarred features that were not improved by an overlarge hooked nose and a receding chin above a mouthful of too-prominent teeth. To make him even more unprepossessing, he was thin with rounded shoulders and bowed legs, even though he had never ridden a horse to create the effect. Nevertheless, despite showing evidence of voluntary neglect, the clothes he was wearing—he had not changed since returning at the conclusion of the display of his weapon—were costly and cut from materials of an excellent quality. His wealth was considerable, having been inherited from a father who combined a brilliant inventive brain with a shrewd head for business. Unlike his son, he had produced several devices of such use that royalty payments of a considerable sum were still regularly forthcoming.

The inability to duplicate his father's abilities in either direction had soured Burke. The disgruntlement over repeated failures to create anything worthwhile had been made worse by the far-from-favorable response that greeted the machine he had felt sure would pick cotton far more efficiently and cheaply than was possible by hand. Being treated with derision by some of those he approached when the problems to which the machine in which he had such faith was prone were made obvious to the potential customers had left him with a deep and lasting hatred for all Southrons, not just those who had done so.

Taking note of the growing hostility between the "slave" and "free" states with not a little satisfaction, although he had no feeling on any of the issues bringing it about, Burke had turned his attention to how he might have his revenge upon the supporters of Secession and, by doing so, also turn a sizable profit his way. Taking note of the rush to acquire weapons of all kinds in the North, especially those that offered the potential to allow the killing of numerous enemies in short periods, he had considered this was the field that could offer him the most scope and started searching for the means to become involved.

About nine months earlier, coming into contact with the metal-cased rounds that were appearing as replacements for paper cartridges—or loading with an individual percussion cap, loose powder, and ball—the less-than-successful inventor had made what he regarded as a most significant breakthrough in the field of firearms manufacture. This had come about from buying the secret of a process and the necessary machinery that allowed brass-cased bullets of a heavier caliber than those currently available for the revolvers already on the market, Smith & Wesson being the most prominent maker and distributor. It had been his intention to patent the process in his own name, having arranged for the designer to be killed in what was accepted as being an accident, then offer to supply the bullets to the major manufacturers of firearms who would have the finance and means to turn out weapons capable of handling them.

Pure chance had led Burke to discover how a firearm could be made to carry out the feeding of a bullet into its chamber, cause it to be discharged, utilize the kick of the recoil to extract the spent case and cock the action, and have all ready for its replacement. Delighted to have arrived at a solution to how he could cause the death of vast numbers of the hated Southrons

by producing a device that would prove even more financially
successful than anything conceived by his father, he had had
no qualms over investing the large sum of money required for
putting the project into effect.

Burke had also been aware of how others involved in the
firearms-manufacturing business would be all too willing to
copy his product without reimbursing him if they could avoid
it. Therefore, he had decided not to take out patents upon his
innovations. Instead, spreading the orders so that no single
manufacturer could guess the purpose to which the various
components would be put, he had acquired them and built
three of the weapons he envisaged. Although they had all
worked, the mechanism operated for only a short time before
the combination of heat and friction from the moving parts
had caused it to malfunction.

Possessing a devious mind and knowledge of how government departments functioned, despite having been unable to
arrive at a solution to the malfunctioning· because he did not
wish to damage either of the remaining pair of guns while
conducting experiments, Burke had not considered that the
problem would prove insurmountable. Instead, he had felt sure
that once military interest was established, he could arrange a
most lucrative deal with the firearms-manufacturing companies
such as Colt, Remington, Sharps, or even the National Armory
at Springfield, Illinois, to take up a license for carrying out the
large-scale production. When the problems came to light, to
avoid the official bungling in discovering it existed earlier becoming known, those responsible for it would insist upon whoever the makers might be to have their technical staff find the
answer to preventing the jamming.

Although an associate in Washington who was under an
obligation to the inventor was successful in causing a depu-
tation from the Army to attend the demonstration of his machine gun, he had been far from impressed by the quality of
the officers who attended it. Instead of the generals he had
thought hearing about a weapon of its quality would bring,
there was only a full colonel—and not even one with experience in warfare as an active participant, which would allow
an appreciation of the firepower it was capable of producing—
in charge of the party. The rest had been majors and captains

also from the Quartermaster Corps or occupying similar non-combatant positions. In his opinion, because of their pacific and never-dangerous occupations, none of them was qualified to render an experienced judgment on the excellence of his most recent brainchild.

What was more, clearly being mere bureaucrats with a disinclination to arrive at decision of any kind than fighting soldiers, none of the party had expressed more than a casual interest in the gun. Rather, the colonel had said vaguely that it could have possibilities and he would report what he had seen to his superiors for them to make the decision regarding its future. Finally, when he had made it apparent that they could not expect any hospitality on his part, the excuse that they must return to Washington without delay was used for them to take their departure.

Having returned to the residence he had rented as offering him the privacy he required for his work, the inventor had had the gun cleaned and put with the remaining ammunition in the cellar until he would be allowed to show it before a more knowledgeable and appreciative audience. Telling his sole assistant to reload the expended cartridges until it was time to finish work for the day, never one to part with his money—although he was still wealthy regardless of his penchant for developing devices that failed to produce the required results when put to the test in actual working conditions—he had given instructions for the man and woman he employed to keep house for him that he would be staying at home and they could leave after she had made his evening meal.

With the food gone, Burke was left alone in the house. However, he had no concern over that. It was, in fact, the way he preferred to be situated, since he was satisfied that there was help within call should the need arise. By arrangement with another of the associates who were financially obligated to him, he had ensured, that this would be the case. The man was commanding officer of a volunteer regiment based near the town while awaiting reaching a strength that would allow them to march off to war. By claiming he was on important official work the nature of which he was not at liberty to disclose, the inventor had had a guard of two men at a time appointed for sentry duty from sundown to sunrise each day.

Their presence had been organized more as a sop for his feelings of neglected self-importance than because he had ever felt protection would be needed. Being of an unsociable nature, he never invited the men assigned to the task to come inside the grounds. However, as he had reported and incurred stiff punishment on a couple who did not stay at their posts, he knew there would not be a repetition of the breach of duty.

Finishing the drink he had poured as a nightcap, the inventor was about to go upstairs and retire for the night when the door to the dining room was thrown open in a violent fashion. With a sensation of alarm, he realized that the four tall, lean, and surly-featured young men who entered were wearing the cadet-gray uniforms of the Confederate States Army, except all were bare-headed. What was more, the swords held by two of them had blood smeared along the blades. It did not need any deep thought for him to know where this had been acquired.

"Wh–wha–what do you w-want?" Burke gasped, staring with growing horror from one to another of the quartet who had burst in upon him.

"That gun of yours," stated the tallest of the four, whose arms bore the triple bars of a sergeant.

"We've a far better use for it than those god-damned fools in the Army would have," the shortest man claimed, waving his blood-smeared saber.

"A whole lot better," the third of the intruders supported. "We're going to make those bastards in Texas wish they'd stayed under Mexican rule instead of joining the Union and then selling us out to the Secessionist scum."

"And that gun of yours is going to do it for us," the fourth man asserted.

Listening to what was said despite his alarm, something began to impinge itself upon Burke's mind. By the time the last remark was made, he realized what was wrong. Although the quartet wore uniforms similar to those he had seen on the few prisoners of war to pass through Glissade, in each case the accent was that of a Northerner with a reasonable education. Nor was his assumption incorrect. Not one of them was a Southern sympathizer, much less a serving member of its Army. In order of their comments, they were Terence Higgins—in no way related to the little Cockney housebreaker who had served Belle Boyd so well—Anthony Whitehead, Frederick Jervis, and Peter Lowe.

The quartet were members of the "liberal" faction who had used political influence to join the United States Secret Service as being safer than serving with the Army in the field, but their mission was not known to any of their superiors, nor—especially where Allan Pinkerton, being a man of honor and far more efficient in his duties than any of them could truthfully claim to be, was concerned—had they any wish for it to be. It was, in fact, a scheme they and a few others of like persuasion had concocted to strike a serious blow at the people of the Confederate States, for whom they had a hatred as pronounced as that of the inventor, albeit founded on even less understandable reasons. The means they were employing had been selected because they felt sure no official sanction for what they planned would be forthcoming; if it became known before its successful completion, it would present the federal government with a fait accompli. Filled with the blind hatred of all their kind for everybody who refused to blindly conform to their ideals and wishes, that the purpose to which the weapons were to be put would cost the lives of numerous innocent women and children did not worry any of them in the least.

"My *gun*?" the inventor croaked, realizing that the intruders were not aware that he had two of the weapons completed and on the premises. "I—I don't know what you me—!"

"You lying, profiteering little bastard!" Jervis yelled, so filled with the exhilaration of having killed with it before entering the grounds that he strode forward and slammed the knuckle bow of his bloodstained sword against the side of Burke's head. "We know all about it even if we weren't invited to the show—!"

The words came to a halt as the speaker saw what the inventor was doing.

Sent to the floor and hurt by the blow, the hatred he always felt toward men larger and better-favored than himself forced an involuntary response from Burke.

Spluttering a profanity, the inventor sent his right hand swiftly into the pocket of his jacket.

Burke had always believed that the work on the weapons

was known only to himself and his assistant, over whom he exerted a control that made exposure extremely unlikely to have taken place. Therefore, although he had never considered that an attempt to steal them would take place, he was aware that the property would strike thieves as a potentially profitable source for robbery. With that contingency in mind, he always had a twin-barreled Derringer pistol suitably sized for concealment and ease of carriage, in the pocket of his jacket and had acquired skill in its use.

Like his companions, Jervis was under the influence of the narcotics they all needed to give them sufficient courage to put their scheme into practice. This and the surge of excited elation he had experienced when driving his sword into the body of one unsuspecting sentry while Whitehead killed the other caused him to respond swiftly to what he realized was a threat to his own existence. Screeching an equally profane exclamation, he went into the kind of lunge he had learned during lessons at fencing. By chance rather than deliberate intent, before the Derringer could be brought clear of the pocket, the point arrived between the inventor's skinny ribs on the left side at a point that it could enter and pierce his heart. His body gave a convulsive jerk and then went limp.

"Thank you, you Yankee *scum*!" said a feminine voice with a Southern accent and redolent of loathing. "You've saved *me* from having to kill him!"

*   *   *

Despite the solution to the threat posed by the weapon she had seen in operation that Belle Boyd had made to Captain Stone Hart, she had had no liking for the thought of what carrying it out would entail. Nevertheless, being able to envisage how great would be the slaughter when examples were manufactured in numbers and employed against members of the Confederate States Army, she had steeled her resolve and had every intention of removing the threat by the means suggested. As a sop to her conscience and with the approval of both Texans when she told them what she hoped to achieve, she said they would burn down wherever the device and its ammunition were being kept along with its inventor, but would not try to find the plans that could be used for producing more of them in the South. Ever a realist, Sergeant Waggles Harrison had claimed it was most unlikely that their people possessed the specialized machinery that would be required to manufacture either the mechanisms or ammunition and he would hate like hell for foreigners to learn how to do so, even if they were willing to supply the finished products to the Confederacy. The girl had found an added solace from the comment.

Remaining in the area from which the undiscovered observation of the demonstration was carried out until the sun went down, Belle and her companions had made their way to a small cabin in another wooded area, where she had arranged for a rendezvous with Doctor Fritz Conried. When she had asked whether it was prudent for him to come, he had assured her that he could leave Glissade without arousing any suspicions. He had established a reputation for taking an occasional night away from his duties to indulge in his genuine hobby of fishing; he preferred to do so alone, on the grounds that it let him get away from people and the problems of their health, which they invariably insisted upon describing in the hope of obtaining free advice.

On being told what had been seen and was intended, Conried had said Belle had arrived at the only possible solution. Sensing her feelings of misgivings about the means to be employed, the doctor had sought to lessen them by telling of what a thoroughly unpleasant and unlikable person Christopher Burke was and described his often virulently expressed bitter hatred for Southrons, which went far beyond feelings of patriotism and belief in the issues that caused the Union to embark in the War. Then he said he would remain where he was until he learned the outcome of the mission. Agreeing with this, the girl had suggested that she and Stone carry it out while Waggles remained with Conried. In that way, should they fail and be caught or killed, the sergeant could take news of this back to Rose Greenhow and allow further measures to prevent the weapons being brought into use to be put into effect. The leathery-faced noncom had been far from enamoured of the part assigned to him, but had grudgingly accepted it as correct.

Taking only one horse apiece, as doing so would arouse less suspicion should they be seen than having two each, Belle

and Stone had set off in accordance with the information supplied by Conried. Stating that he felt honor-bound to do so
and that its cadet-gray color would not be discernible in the
darkness, the Captain had changed into his Confederate uniform. Accepting the decision without hesitation or qualms, to
allow the greatest possible ease of movement, the girl was
wearing her man's black shirt, riding breeches, and boots. Like
Stone, she had on the military weapon belt and its personal
armament. However, as the unusual design of the girl's *épée
de combat* was unlikely to be noticed in the poor light, it was
determined that these would give credence to their being nothing more than a pair of Union soldiers going about lawful
activity.

Having been told by the doctor what little to expect by way
of defenses, Belle and Stone had settled upon how they could
gain admittance on arrival at the small house. Although steeled
in their resolve over how Burke must be dealt with, neither
had wanted the death of the two sentries added to the toll
regardless of their being nominal enemies. Therefore, they had
elected to make use of the drugged whiskey that had served
them so well against the three Yankee cavalrymen. They found
the pair dead from what had clearly been unexpected thrusts
by some kind of edged weapons, but circumstances had not
permitted a sufficiently close examination to establish what
these might be.

However, as the pair felt sure that no other Confederate
supporters had been assigned to perform a similar mission to
their own, they had assumed nothing more than that armed
thieves were responsible for the killing. With that in mind,
they had left their horses with the four already standing hitched
to rings in the walls surrounding the property and advanced
on foot. Having no doubt that they would meet resistance when
putting in their appearance, sharing what they guessed from
the corpses was a reluctance on the part of the men responsible
to be a realization that the use of firearms could attract un-
wanted attention and investigation, they had left their revolvers
holstered and intended to rely on cold steel for their protection.

Having heard the conversation that took place and noticing
the obviously Northern accents of the speakers, Stone finding
the reference to the very adverse effect upon Texas of what-

ever was planned for using the guns of especial interest, he and Belle knew that they were not up against other supporters of the Southern cause regardless of the attire worn by the four men. However, Belle in particular found the sight of Frederick Jervis killing the inventor something of a relief, as his death removed the necessity for her—and she had been determined that it was she, not the honorable soldier she knew the Texan to be, who must carry out what was going to be a cold-blooded execution—to do so. In spite of this, she could not prevent herself from announcing their presence by making the statement that came as a shock to the men in the room.

"*Rebs*!" Anthony Whitehead screeched rather than yelled, staring in an alarm that was duplicated by his companions at the two figures that came through the door. Stone's uniform was evidence of where his loyalties lay in the War Between the States. However, although offering no such indication of her allegiance, Belle's snugly fitting attire established her sex beyond a doubt, and like her reference to "Yankee scum," her accent was sufficient to prove that she, too, was a Southern supporter. "Kill them!"

The same idea had already struck the other three "liberals." Thinking and moving more quickly than Terence Higgins, for all his insistence upon wearing the stripes of a sergeant—because he considered himself to be their leader on account of having thought up the scheme that had brought them to Burke's residence—selecting the beautiful slenderly curvaceous girl on the assumption that she would be the least dangerous of the intruders, Frederick Jones and Peter Lowe darted toward her. Arriving at the same conclusion, Whitehead followed them with an equal alacrity. Much to his perturbation, the tallest of the quartet found himself left to face the grim-featured Confederate officer. He possessed some skill at fencing, but soon discovered he was up against an opponent with even greater skill.

Finding herself being approached by three men armed with swords, Belle was able to draw some consolation from the room having been made large enough for use during the frequently well-attended functions given by the previous owners. Having no such desire for company, especially when it would be at his own expense, Burke had had the furnishings reduced to the small table with just two chairs at which he took his meals in the center, a settee, and a few other small items placed around the walls. This gave her the room she required to maneuver, and she began to take advantage of it. What was more, the skill she possessed was sufficient to prevent her from becoming the easy victim her attackers believed would prove the case. It quickly became apparent that none of them even came close to matching her ability.

Far from finding the girl the easy prey they had envisaged, the three "liberals" soon discovered that they were in contention against an extremely competent antagonist. Not only did the blade of the *épée de combat* fend off their attempt at striking her, aided by the trio's getting into one another's way in their eagerness to kill her, she soon found an opportunity to put to use part of the instruction she had received from Captain Anatol de-Farge in unfair fighting.

Deftly snapping up her left leg while beating away the opposing blades, despite its arriving with much less force than she would have been able to apply under less pressing conditions, the savate kick that the girl delivered to Lowe's crotch was sufficient to send him staggering back a few steps, registering pain without totally incapacitating him. A moment later, while knocking aside Whitehead's blade with the side of her left arm, there was none of the attempts to avoid striking a mortal blow that had been employed during the fight in her sitting room on the night her parents died and her home was burned to the ground. Now, knowing it to be a matter of life or death, she fought with savage and deadly intent. This showed as she went into a lunge that sent her own point into Jervis's left breast. Although this was a fatal stroke, she realized she would not be able to withdraw the weapon in time to prevent Whitehead's resuming the deflected attack.

Even as Belle was starting to pull free the *épée de combat*, she received succor. Delivering a close-to-classic "cut at head" attack that almost severed all the way through its recipient's neck, Stone saw her deadly predicament. Allowing the nearly decapitated body of Higgins to fall aside without giving it a second glance, knowing no further effort need be expended in that direction, he darted toward the girl and her attacker. Even as he was sending the blade of his saber into

Whitehead's back so its point inflicted a mortal wound, Lowe returned to the fray.

Although starting from so far away that only the tip made contact, the Yankee's sword tore a gash down the right side of the Texan's cheek. An instant later, still not showing the slightest hesitation in her response or seeking to soften its effect, she executed a downward "cut at head" and the last of the quartet met his end. With Belle's right hand turned in half pronation, the razor-sharp blade of the *épée de combat* struck the top of Lowe's skull. Such was the excellent quality of the steel that it bit through hair and bone to reach the brain. Killed outright, he crumpled to the floor and lay without movement. For a moment, with a shudder shaking Belle's slender frame and perspiration flowing freely down her face, the two victors of the fight stood looking about them to ensure there would be no further need for defense against the quartet.

"We have to get you to Doctor Conried so he can attend to your wound, Stone!" the girl stated, regaining her composure as she looked at the bleeding gash running down her companion's right cheek.

"Not until we've done what we came here for," the Texan answered, his voice giving an indication of the pain he was suffering as he clasped the napkin that Burke had used during the evening meal. "I hope we can burn this place down so completely that there's nothing to suggest we Southrons killed him."

* * *

"This has to be stitched, Captain Hart," Doctor Fritz Conried declared, having examined the injury sustained by the Texan in the light of the small lantern that was supplying the illumination he had claimed was safe provided they listened for anybody who might be approaching. "The cut did not go all the way through your cheek, but it very nearly has and there is no other way I can treat it."

A search of Christopher Burke's house by Belle Boyd and her companion, who had continued to try to staunch the blood from the wound while doing so, had provided them with the means to accomplish their purpose. There had been sufficient kerosene in one portion of the cellar to ensure a conflagration that would cause the property to be burned to the ground as totally as Baton Royale Manor had been on the night her parents were murdered. Furthermore, her skill at picking locks had given them access to the section in which the weapons, a supply of ammunition, powder, and a supply of lead for reloading the spent cases and machinery were stored.

Because Stone was in considerable pain and less than steady on his feet as the result of the loss of blood, the work of arson had been by the girl. She had done so with such effect that, as they rode away leading the four horses upon which the quartet of ''liberals'' had arrived and were to be released when clear of the property, they knew there was no way the fire could be halted before it completed the destruction they desired. This had been even more certain when they heard the explosion caused when the flames reached the gunpowder. In fact, when Conried reported the aftermath of the affair some time later, they discovered that not a trace of their activities remained and the general consensus of opinion among those who investigated the destruction of the property was that it came about due to an accidental fire. The doctor had concluded by saying that he believed the loss of the weapon had been something of a relief to those members of the Union Army who would have had to take time and spend money checking its potential as an addition to their cause's already extensive weaponry.

In spite of the pain he was enduring even after the flow of blood was staunched by its congealment, Stone had ridden with Belle back to the cabin where Sergeant Waggles Harrison and Conried were waiting. For all his eagerness to be given a verbal report of what had happened, the doctor had insisted upon attending to the wound while this was given by the girl. The removal of the napkin, which was now stiffened with the congealed blood, had been the cause of more suffering for the Captain. However, he and the others realized there would be more to come as a result of the treatment that it was necessary to have performed.

''Go to it, Doc!'' Stone authorized through gritted teeth.

''It isn't that easy,'' Conried warned. ''I've got sutures and needles in my bag, but anesthetic of all kinds is in such short supply to us civilian practitioners that, as I didn't anticipate any would be needed, I daren't chance bringing along any of my small supply. I'm sorry, but—!''

"You weren't to know," Stone stated. "So I'll just have to do without."

"If it was only that easy!" the doctor sighed. "You're going to be hurt more than a little by the stitching, and we've no way of reducing the pain."

"We've the opiate in the whiskey," Belle pointed out.

"That would do," Conried admitted, but his voice was redolent of misgivings. "But, from what you told me of its effects and taking Captain Hart's condition into account, it might render him unconscious for hours."

"And we don't have hours to spare, Belle," the Captain asserted. "Likely they'll be hunting around for whoever started the fire, and we all have to be long gone before they do. So do you best get her done, Doc. Waggles can hold me still."

"I doubt whether he, or any other man, could do it, the suffering you'll be put through," Conried denied, and his gaze went to Belle. "But, from what I know about the stubborn sense of masculine pride I'm sure you'll have, Captain Hart, a *woman* might be able to let you endure it."

"Then a *woman* is going to do the holding," the girl declared, and although her upbringing at the hands of her mother and Auntie Mattie Jonias had no liking for the decision she had made, she started to remove her shirt to leave her bare to the waist. Taking the wounded officer's hands in her own and positioning herself so that her bare breasts would be within his range of vision, she went on, "And you're going to know for *certain* that it is a woman holding you, Stone."

None of the men realized that they were witnessing another example of the lengths to which Belle Boyd would go in meeting the needs of an assignment.

When the girl became known as the Rebel Spy, nobody who knew the way she had acquired the fame that brought this about would claim the sobriquet was undeserved.

PART FOUR

THE DECISION

"Hello, Professor 'Zac," Belle Boyd said as the elderly man who was the sole occupant of the room she had entered started to rise from the desk at which he was working. Gesturing to the sheets of paper lying before him, she continued, "Is this something of interest?"

"It could be, my dear," replied Wladystaw Smreczak, the difficulty most people who did not share his Polish birthright found in trying to pronounce his full name having resulted in the abbreviation used by the girl. Waving one sheet of the papers, he elaborated, "This is a message in code from a Yankee spy which our Lady has received, and I'm trying to decipher it."

Although Captain Stone Hart had clearly been suffering through the journey, Belle and the Texans had experienced no difficulty in returning to Confederate-held territory after having parted company with Doctor Fritz Conried. Accompanying her to Arlington in accordance with the instructions received from Rose Greenhow before setting off on the mission, by the kind of coincidence no author would dare use in a work of fiction, Stone had his injury examined by her friend Phillipe Front de Bouef, who was now a captain and surgeon for the garrison in the town. Despite saying the suturing of the gash had been performed in an excellent fashion and it was healing correctly, Front de Boeuf had warned that it would nevertheless leave a livid white scar down the otherwise tanned right cheek, which would mar the Texan's handsome features permanently.

After assuring Belle that they did not hold her responsible for what had happened, Stone and Sergeant Harrison were thanked by Rose on behalf of the General Staff for their participation. Warned no mention of the mission could be put on their military records for obvious reasons, they had set off to rejoin their regiment, wherein they continued to serve with distinction until the cessation of hostilities caused them to take up another career. However, before leaving, Stone had asked Rose and Belle to do all they could to find out the nature of the scheme that could threaten the welfare of Texas. Despite all their organization could do, they failed, and it was not until a few years later that the truth became known.[1]

Much to the girl's relief, on hearing what had taken place during the mission, her aunt had stated approval with everything that had taken place. Rose had said that, while it was necessary to prevent the potentially lethal weapon from reaching the Union Army, she was pleased the execution of Christopher Burke had not needed to be carried out by her niece. She had also declared that she would ensure that no blame was placed on the party for failing to bring away either of the devices or the plans for their manufacture.

When told about the gun later, being something of an expert on the subject, Captain Alexandre Dartagnan had said its not being available for reproduction by the South would be of no great disadvantage. He had duplicated the assumption by Stone Hart regarding the malfunctions that had occurred and claimed overcoming the problem would cost much time and money better employed for other purposes. On the other hand, he had asserted that some other inventor would eventually come up with a similar solution to producing a gun that would operate without the need of manual cranking and the means to stop the jamming due to friction. Belle had concurred with his wish that such a development would not come into the hands of the North, and they both lived long enough to see the first types of genuine machine guns designed by Hiram Percy Maxim and John Moses Browning, among others, brought into service around the world.

Having been told by Rose to rest, since there could be another assignment taking her into Union territory forthcoming, Belle had been only too willing to do this; she was tired as a result of the one she had just successfully accomplished. Having found herself at a loose end and being on friendly terms with Professor 'Zac, hearing he had arrived from Richmond

[1] *What the scheme was and how it came to be implemented is told in* THE DEVIL GUN.

in response to a summons from her aunt, she had decided to drop by and see him. Always willing to take an interest in everything that might improve her efficiency as a spy, she crossed to the desk and looked at the paper he was placing before him to resume his work.

"It's a numeral substitution, I see," Belle remarked.

"Yes," the elderly Polish expert answered. "And they can be *most* difficult to break unless one has the key."

"Perhaps the Yankees have used the same kind of key wording as we did," the girl suggested. "Why not see whether they've used the first lines of 'Dixie' as the base."

"It's worth a try," Professor 'Zac admitted, and took another sheet of paper. Having written "Southrons hear your country call you, up lest death or worse befall you, to arms, to arms, to arms in Dixie" and placed numbers from one to twenty-six above the appropriate letters, he compared the result with the message and shook his head. "No, that isn't it."

"They might not know the General's words," Belle pointed out. "Or considered them too patriotic to be used."

"That's possible," the expert conceded, and carried out a similar test with "I wish I was in the land of cotton, old days there are not forgotten, look away, look away, away down south in Dixie," written by Daniel D. Emmet.

"I wonder if they might have decided it would be too obvious and used 'Yankee Doodle' like we do?" Belle remarked, after another experiment failed to produce anything understandable.

The first attempt to employ the numbers used by the Confederate States Secret Service proved no more successful than the preceding pair. However, Professor 'Zac had an inspiration. Reversing the order of the numbers, he found that he was able to reproduce the message in its entirety. Reading what he printed neatly on another sheet of paper, he raised his head and looked hard at Belle.

"Look at *this*!" the elderly expert requested.

"So this is where they are going to be in five days!" the girl breathed as she did as requested. The message was addressed to the names by which George Tollinger and Alfred Barmain were now known and instructed them to attend a rendezvous with other agents of the Yankee Secret Service at

Grunion, a town she had never heard of. Checking the map on the wall of the office, she found it to be a small place on the way to Brandywine and estimated the distance to be no more than five miles over the Pennsylvania border. Her face lost all its color as she gritted rather than just said, "Excuse me, please, Professor 'Zac. I must show this to my aunt immediately."

"I knew you would, my dear," the expert replied. "And good luck to you."

"Ah, Belle," Rose greeted as the girl entered her room. She was holding a sheet of paper and looked grim. "I was just about to send for you—!"

"I know where Tollinger and Barmain are," Belle interrupted before her aunt could say any more. "They're less than five miles away, at Grunion!"

"And this information has to be taken to our people in Annapolis as quickly as possible," Rose pointed out, aware that the town she named was in the opposite direction to where her niece mentioned. "It's in the opposite direction to Grunion."

"I *know* that!" Belle admitted in a bitter tone.

"There's nobody else I could send who knows the route as well as you," Rose stated. "Or who stands your chance of getting through. If there was, I wouldn't ask you to go under the circumstances."

For several seconds, Belle looked into her aunt's face. Conflicting thoughts churned through her. The men whom she had seen murder her mother and father were close by, and she was confident that she could reach them to wreak the revenge she had sworn to take. On the other hand, when she had enrolled in Rose Greenhow's organization, she had taken upon herself a duty to the Confederate States that overrode considerations of personal vengeance. Furthermore, she had sworn on the name of her parents that she would never allow thoughts of taking revenge upon Tollinger and Barmain stand between her and her duty.

Never had Belle faced such a dilemma.

If she took on the delivery of the information, the girl might never again be so close to the two men for whom she felt such bitter hatred and they might escape her for all time.

Should she decline the task and seek personal revenge?

Or should she do her duty as an agent for the Confederate States and deliver the information, even though carrying out this would almost certainly result in Tollinger and Barmain escaping?

There was, Belle knew, only one decision she could reach if she wanted to uphold the promise she had made to Rose the night they met. Raised in the rigid Southern code of conduct, which they had taught her to follow, Electra and Vincent Boyd would expect it of her. Furthermore, if she should refuse the assignment, she would never be able to look herself in the face again even if she achieved her desire to take revenge on Tollinger and Barmain. What was more, she would be honor-bound to tender her resignation and be finished as a member of the South's Secret Service.

"Give me the message," the girl said after drawing in a deep breath and standing stiff as a bar of steel. "And I'll get it there!"

"I knew you would say that!" Rose claimed, looking at Belle with pride and knowing full well what giving the agreement had cost. "It's what I would expect of one who is already gaining a name among the Yankees as a Rebel Spy!"

Appendix

Wanting a son and learning his wife, Electra, could not have any more children, Vincent Charles Boyd gave his only daughter, Belle,[1] a thorough training in several subjects not normally regarded as being necessary for the upbringing of a wealthy Southron girl. At seventeen she could ride—astride or sidesaddle—as well as any of her male neighbors, men who were to help provide the Confederate States with its superlative cavalry. In addition, she was a skilled performer with an *épée de combat* or a sabre,[2] an excellent shot with any kind of firearm, and an expert at *savate*, the French style of foot and fist boxing. All these accomplishments were to be very useful to her as time went by.

Shortly before the commencement of the War Between the States, a mob of pro-Union supporters led by two "liberal" agitators who fled north immediately after stormed the Boyd plantation. Before they were driven off by the girl and the family's Negro servants, they had murdered her parents and burned her home to the ground. On recovering from the wound she sustained in the fighting, hostilities having broken out between the South and the North, she joined the successful spy ring organized by her aunt, Rose Greenhow.[3] Wanting to find and take revenge upon the leaders of the mob, Belle was not

[1] *According to the world's foremost fictionist genealogist, Philip Jose Farmer, author of, among numerous other works,* TARZAN ALIVE, *the Definitive Biography of Lord Greystoke and* DOC SAVAGE, *His Apocalyptic Life—with whom we have consulted, Belle Boyd was the grand-aunt of Jane, Lady Greystoke, nee Porter, whose biography is recorded in the* TARZAN OF THE APES *series by Edgar Rice Burroughs.*
[2] *An épée de combat is used mainly for thrusting and the sabre was originally intended chiefly for slashing from the back of a horse.*
[3] *One incident in Rose Greenhow's career is recorded in:* KILL DUSTY FOG!

content to operate in one locality. Instead, she undertook the dangerous task of delivering other agents' information to the appropriate Confederate authorities. Adding an ability at disguise and in producing different dialects to her other accomplishments, she graduated to handling even more important and risky assignments, attaining such proficiency that she won the sobriquet "the Rebel Spy." On two missions she worked with Captain Dustine Edward Marsden "Dusty" Fog, Company "C," Texas Light Cavalry.[4] Another had first brought her into contact with the Ysabel Kid[5] and later, in his company, she had concluded her quest of vengeance upon the men responsible for the murder of her parents.[6]

While the "Yankees" were given reason to hate the Rebel Spy when she was engaged in her duties against them during the war, the majority had no cause to feel other than gratitude after peace was brought about by the meeting at the Appomattox Court House. On signing the oath of allegiance to the Union, she was enrolled in the United States Secret Service. Despite all the trouble she had given that organization throughout the hostilities, she served it loyally and with equal efficiency. Her participation in thwarting a plot to assassinate President Ulysses Simpson Grant prevented friction and possibly another war between the Southern and Northern States.[7] Assisted by Martha "Calamity Jane" Canary[8] and Belle

---

[4] *Told in* THE COLT AND THE SABRE *and* THE REBEL SPY.
[5] *Told in* THE BLOODY BORDER.

5a. Details of Captain Dustine Edward Marsden "Dusty" Fog's and the Ysabel Kid's careers are given in the Civil War *and* Floating Outfit *series.*
[6] *Told in* BACK TO THE BLOODY BORDER.
[7] *Told in* THE HOODED RIDERS.
[8] *Information regarding the career of Martha "Calamity Jane" Canary is to be found in the* Calamity Jane *series and she makes "guest" appearances in Part One, "The Bounty on Belle Starr's Scalp," TROUBLED RANGE; its "expansion," CALAMITY, MARK AND BELLE; Part One, "Better Than Calamity," THE WILDCATS; THE BAD BUNCH; THE FORTUNE HUNTERS; Part Six, "Mrs. Wild Bill," J. T.'S LADIES; Part Four, "Draw Poker's Such a Simple Game," J. T.'S LADIES RIDE AGAIN ("costarring" with the lady outlaw Belle Starr); Part Seven, "Deadwood, August the 2nd, 1876, J. T.'S HUNDEDTH; Part*

Starr,[9] she brought to an end the reign of terror caused by a murderous gang of female outlaws.[10] With the aid of the OD Connected ranch's floating outfit, she broke up the Brotherhood for Southern Freedom.[11] In the same company she prevented diplomatic difficulties between the United States and Haiti.[12] She joined forces once more with Belle Starr and the Ysabel Kid when involved in the efforts of the international

Four, "A Wife for Dusty Fog," THE SMALL TEXAN and GUNS IN THE NIGHT.

[9a] Belle Starr makes "guest" appearances in RANGELAND HERCULES; THE BAD BUNCH; DIAMONDS, EMERALDS, CARDS AND COLTS; THE CODE OF DUSTY FOG; THE GENTLE GIANT; HELL IN THE PALO DURO; GO BACK TO HELL; Part Four, "A Lady Known As Belle," THE HARD RIDERS; Part Two, "We Hang Horse Thieves High," J. T.'S HUNDREDTH and Part Six, "Mrs. Wild Bill," J. T.'S LADIES. The circumstances of her death are told in GUNS IN THE NIGHT.

[9b] The lady outlaw "stars," no pun intended, in WANTED! BELLE STARR.

[9c] We are frequently asked why it is the "Belle Starr" we describe is so different from a photograph that appears in various books. The researches of Philip Jose Farmer, q.v., have established the lady for whom we are biographer is not the same person as another equally famous bearer of the name. However, the Counter family has asked Mr. Farmer and ourselves to keep her true identity a secret and this we intend to do.

[10] Told in THE BAD BUNCH.

[11] Told in TO ARMS! TO ARMS! IN DIXIE and THE SOUTH WILL RISE AGAIN.

[11a] "Floating outfit": a group of four to six cowhands employed by a large ranch to work the more distant sections of the property. Taking food in a chuck wagon, or "greasy sack" on the back of a mule, they would be away from the ranch house for long periods and so were selected for their honesty, loyalty, reliability, and capability in all aspects of their work. Because of the owner of the OD Connected ranch, General Jackson Baines "Ole Devil" Hardin's prominence in the affairs of Texas, members of its floating outfit were frequently sent to assist such of his friends who found themselves in difficulties or endangered.

[11b] Details of the career of General Jackson Baines "Ole Devil" Hardin are given in the Ole Devil Hardin, Civil War and Floating Outfit series; also Part Four, "Mr. Colt's Revolving Cylinder Pistol," J. T.'S HUNDREDTH. His death is reported in DOC LEROY, M.D.

[12] Told in SET A-FOOT.

master criminal Octavius Xavier "the Ox" Guillemot to gain possession of James Bowie's knife.[13] Working with Calamity Jane and Captain Patrick Reeder of the British Secret Service, she wrecked two attempts by European anarchists to create hostility between the U.S.A. and Great—as it was *then*—Britain.[14] Assisted by the successful British lady criminal Amelia Penelope Diana "Benkers" Benkinsop, she dealt with the man who had sold arms to the plotters.[15]

[13] *Told in* THE QUEST FOR BOWIE'S BLADE.

[14] *Told in* THE REMITTANCE KID *and* THE WHIP AND THE WAR LANCE.

[14a] *The researches of Philip Jose Farmer, q.v., have established that Captain Patrick Reeder (later Major General Sir, K.C.B, VC, D.S.O., MC and Bar) was the uncle of the celebrated British detective, Mr. Jeremiah Golden Reeder, whose biography appears in* ROOM 13, THE MIND OF MR. J. G. REEDER, RED ACES, MR. J. G. REEDER RETURNS, THE GUV'NOR *and* TERROR KEEP *by Edgar Wallace.*

[14b] *Mr. Jeremiah Golden Reeder's organization plays a prominent part in the events we recorded as* "CAP" FOG, TEXAS RANGER, MEET MR. J. G. REEDER; THE RETURN OF RAPIDO CLINT AND MR. J. G. REEDER *and* RAPIDO CLINT STRIKES BACK.

[15] *Told in* Part Five, "The Butcher's Fiery End," J. T.'S LADIES.

[15a] *Some other activities of the very competent British lady criminal Amelia Penelope Diana "Benkers" Benkinsop during her visit to the United States in the mid-1870s are recorded in* BEGUINAGE IS DEAD! *and* Part Three, "Birds of a Feather," WANTED! BELLE STARR.

[15b] *Information about a descendant of the above "Benkers"—who also followed the family tradition of retaining the full name regardless of who the father might be—Miss Amelia Penelope Diana Benkinsop, G. C., M.A., B.Sc. (Oxon.), owner of Benkinsop's Academy for the Daughters of Gentlefolk in England, is given in* BLONDE GENIUS; Part One, "Fifteen The Hard Way," J. T.'S LADIES *and* Part Two, "A Case of Blackmail," J. T.'S LADIES RIDE AGAIN.

[15c] BLONDE GENIUS *is the rarest of our books. To date, copies which have passed through the hands of the* J. T. EDSON APPRECIATION SOCIETY *and have been auctioned by us for charity have realized from avid collectors: £60.00; U.S. $65.00; £35.00; U.S. $30.00 and three at £25.00 each.*